THE GIRLS
OF CANBY HALL®

SUMMER
BLUES

THE GIRLS
OF CANBY HALL®

THE GIRLS OF CANBY HALL®

SUMMER BLUES

EMILY CHASE

SCHOLASTIC INC.
New York Toronto London Auckland Sydney

ISBN 0-590-33237-6

12 11 10 9 8 7 6 5 4 3   5 6 7 8 9/8

Printed in the U.S.A.   06

CHAPTER ONE

Shelley sat at her desk by the window, face propped in her hands, looking out over the campus of Canby Hall.

It was only a week before final exams, but the June day outside was too distracting to study through. It was impossible to focus on geometry when everyone else was outside enjoying the afternoon — laughing, talking, spinning Frisbees at each other. The damp grass was letting off its greeny scent in the sunlight. And the grassy smell was mixing with the fragrance of the pink and white flowers bordering the walks, and the smell of tanning lotion on the girls lying on towels on the front lawn of Baker House. Sprinklers were hissing. Fat bees were buzzing. It might technically still be spring term, but summer had clearly arrived in Greenleaf, Massachusetts.

Amazing, Shelley thought. Only two weeks left until the end of the school year. When

1

she came here last September, she thought
just making it until Christmas would be a
nearly impossible endurance test. And now
here she was, planning to stay on for the
optional summer term. Of course, she was a
very different person from the one who had
arrived here nine months ago from Pine
Bluff, Iowa. The chubby, small-town girl,
whose older brothers called her "Slugger"
(after a disastrous childhood start at playing
baseball), now had ten fewer pounds on her
frame, pierced ears, and a hot new haircut.
The girl who had wanted to grow up to be a
happy homemaker like her mother was now
determined to become one of America's great
actresses. Last fall's hopelessly-devoted-to-
hometown-Paul girl, who wanted to settle
down as soon as possible into a long, long
marriage like her parents had, was now jug-
gling two boyfriends at the same time.
Oooooo. Sometimes it made Shelley's head
hurt just trying to think about her romantic
dilemma.

A huge crash saved her from her thoughts.
She turned with a start to see her roommate
Faith sprawled in the now open doorway to
their room. She was wearing satin shorts, a
tank top, and roller skates.

"You'll get probation for sure if they catch
you practicing in the halls," Shelley said,
rushing over, hauling Faith up by her arm-
pits. With eight spinning wheels on her feet,
Faith was having trouble getting a grip on

the planet Earth. Her legs just kept flailing away as Shelley dragged her over to the closest bed in the dorm room.

"It . . . uh . . . doesn't say . . . argh . . . anything about . . . roller-skating in the . . . ugh . . . handbook," Faith grunted and gasped as she was being dragged across the room.

"That's only because they couldn't imagine anyone being so weird as to try it in the dorm," Shelley said, dumping Faith onto the mattress. "I thought black people were supposed to be more coordinated. Where's all that natural rhythm?" Shelley said, teasingly.

This was another very big change. When they moved into this room — 407 Baker House — last fall, Faith was so suspicious of Shelley that she would never have taken a tease like this. The two of them had come through a lot to understand, love, and trust each other as they did now.

"I'm only coordinated when I'm on terra firma," Faith replied. "I guess this ends my hopes for a big career in the roller derby. At least I tried it out in private, and didn't have to make a complete fool of myself in front of the entire population of Canby Hall."

When Faith arrived last fall from Washington, D.C., where she lived with her mother, a social worker; her older sister Sarah; and younger brother Richard, she was a closed-up person. When her father, a police officer, got shot and killed five years before, trying to stop a robbery, Faith cried for a long time. When she stopped, she decided she didn't want to cry anymore for the rest of her life, and so she sealed off her emotions behind a stone wall. The past months of caring and fun and friendship with Shelley and their roommate, Dana, had done a lot to break down that wall, though.

Faith leaned over, looked out the window, and nodded at the lawn below. "Is that Dana down there soaking up those prime rays? Remind me to add tanning to my list of amazing things white folks do for fun."

"Did she decide if she's going to stay for the summer intensive yet?" Shelley asked. "I hate the thought of this great trio of roommates breaking up, even just for the summer."

Faith was bent over her long thin legs, undoing the laces on her skates and pulling them off. "Oh, she's still debating, but seeing as Bret's staying around, my guess is that she'll be here. Plus, I've just heard that the poetry intensive is going to be given by none other than the famous, the one and only. . . ."

"Not *Grace Phaeton*!" Shelley shrieked. "Oh, void! Oh, dark abyss, vortex of the shriveled soul!" She put her hand over her heart and hopped up on a chair to impersonate Dana reciting one of Grace Phaeton's lines.

Both Faith and Shelley thought Grace Phaeton's poems were the most depressing stuff in modern literature, but Dana was wild about her. No amount of sarcasm from her two roommates—not even the time they both pretended to write suicide notes when she began reading aloud one night — made the smallest dent in Dana's admiration.

"Well," Faith said. "You're right, girl. If Gracey baby is teaching here this summer, Dana will definitely stick around."

They nodded at each other and smiled. They had already decided to stay on for intensives, and things wouldn't be as much fun without Dana there.

Intensives were a big deal around Canby Hall. They ran from late June to late July and were essentially a month's immersion in a single area. This year they were being offered in drama, art, photography, poetry, and dance. Each intensive was taught by a professional in the subject, sometimes a big name. Another interesting feature of intensives was that they were a joint program with Oakley Prep, the boys school nearby.

Faith's consuming interest was photography, and so there was no way she'd miss taking an intensive in it. It would also give her an extra month with her boyfriend, Johnny Bates, who lived in Greenleaf, the nearest town to campus.

For Shelley, the drama intensive looked to be not only a great professional opportunity, but also a possible solution to her romantic problem. Specifically, the two-boyfriend problem. There was Tom who went to Greenleaf High here, and Paul back home, neither of whom knew about the other. This would give her the chance to divide the summer between the two of them. *And* the chance to take acting from André Rosofsky, the famous New York drama coach.

Once Faith had gotten free of her skates, she and Shelley decided it was too beautiful an afternoon to spend it inside. They opened the bottom of Shelley's piggy bank to see if there was enough for banana splits at Tutti Frutti in Greenleaf. While they were counting out change on the floor, Dana walked in. Or rather someone who looked a lot like Dana, but also a lot like a lobster in a bikini.

"Oh, no!" Shelley exclaimed when she saw this sight.

"Girl," Faith said, appraising Dana in her usual calm, laidback way, "you have really gone and done it, I'm afraid. I'll go down to the infirmary and try to pry some burn ointment out of Nurse Zinger. Shel, why don't you sit Miss Medium Rare in a cold tub, to take out some of the sting?"

"How did you do this?" Shelley asked Dana, who was still standing in the doorway, looking afraid to find out what moving would feel like.

"I fell asleep. I just woke up. I don't feel too bad actually. Just a little crispy. But I've got a feeling it's going to get a lot worse."

"That's what happens to a chic New York City girl when she gets out of her element.

You just don't know anything about nature," Shelley said.

"Don't worry, Dana," Faith said. "You've come to the right place — 407 Baker Crisis Center. We'll take care of you. *Plus*, we've got a little news flash that might make you forget you look like a piece of bacon."

"What?"

"Three guesses," Shelley said.

"Come *on*. No fair. Here I am suffering and you two are making me play game show contestant!"

"Here's your clue," Faith said, slipping past Dana on her way down to the infirmary, pressing the palm of one hand to her heart, the back of the other hand to her forehead — a high-drama gesture. "Oh, burning wonder! Oh, crimson flame! Oh, lost soul in search of Solarcaine!"

CHAPTER TWO

I'm not giving out any medication to go,"
Nurse Zinger told Faith. "This is an infirmary, not a McDonald's."

And then she picked up the phone and
called Alison Cavanaugh, the housemother
at Baker.

"I hear you've got a bad case of sunburn
over there."

This was the first Alison had heard of it.

"Who?" she asked.

"Dana Morrison."

Alison gasped. "I'll check right into it,"
she told Nurse Zinger. Then she hung up
and ran up the four flights to Dana's room.
Although there was a ten-year difference between their ages, and although Alison was
Dana's housemother, the two of them considered themselves real friends. And so Alison was upset to hear that something was
wrong with Dana, doubly upset that no one
had told her about it.

By the time she got up to the room, Alison was panting and looking even wilder than she usually did. She was a tall young woman with long, tumbling, reddish-brown hair and big horn-rimmed glasses that were perpetually sliding down off the bridge of her nose. She wore clothes that were more earth mother than housemother — peasant skirts and rough woven tops and scarves of many bright colors.

The door to 407 was open, so Alison just barreled in and didn't stop until she saw Dana.

"Oh, kiddo!" she said. "I hurt just looking at you!" And then, without a moment's hesitation, she told Dana, "We're putting you in the infirmary."

"You think it's serious?" Dana asked. She was beginning to worry at all this attention.

"No, I don't. But Zinger's got the supplies and the know-how over there to make you feel better. You look like you might have a time of it tonight. I just want you to get through this as easily as possible."

It *was* a rough night. Every time Dana tried to turn over, or move anything, she hurt. A couple of times during the night, Nurse Zinger came in to apply cold wet cloths to the burns, which helped. Toward morning, Dana fell into a deep sleep for a couple of hours and woke to find that she didn't hurt quite as much.

She got up and looked at herself in the mirror over the sink opposite the bed. The long brown hair and bright green eyes were the same as ever, but everything else looked different, and not better-different. Her lips and eyes were puffed up. Her nose looked like Rudolph's. Her skin was pulled tight and shone in the light from the lamp above the mirror.

"I think the worst is over," she told Faith and Shelley when they came down before dashing off to classes. "Zinger says I'll live. But I have to stay the day. I think she's lonesome. I'm her only patient."

"Where is she now?" Faith asked. "Boiling up a cauldron of bat wing and eye of newt for you?" Nurse Zinger was a surly woman with a large, hooked nose and so had been kiddingly compared to a witch for as long as she had been at Canby Hall.

"To tide you over until lunch," Shelley said, dropping a Snickers bar and a copy of *Soap Opera Digest* on Dana's bed.

"Yeah," Faith added. "Don't eat anything Zinger brings. Especially if it's foaming."

After her roommates left, Dana did some Spanish homework, read a little of the magazine, then drifted off to sleep thinking about her boyfriend, Bret, fantasizing about him rushing to her bedside with flowers.

She had asked Faith and Shelley not to call him about her sunburn. She didn't want to seem like a wimp or overdramatize a small thing. But she did wish he'd trip on to the news that she was in the infirmary.

But he hadn't called in several days now. Dana had to admit to herself that he hadn't been calling as much as he used to. She had been trying not to notice this. She wanted things to keep going as perfectly as they had been. Having wrested Bret away from all the other girls at Canby Hall last fall, she had been traveling on a gauzy cloud of love through the whole school year.

Having Bret around had done a lot to ease the trauma Dana had gone through over her father. She had been hoping that he and her mother would get back together, even though they had been officially divorced for a while. But he had put a fast end to those hopes this year by planning on marrying Eve the next month — Eve, who seemed too young to Dana to be her stepmother. Eventually, she had come to accept and even like Eve, but there were some rough patches along the way, and if Bret hadn't been there, they would have been a lot rougher.

And now, with Grace Phaeton teaching the poetry intensive, she would ask her mother if she could stay. Her mother, who was a buyer in a New York department store, would be working anyway and wouldn't mind. That would mean Dana and Bret would have a romantic month of summer together.

And then next year, Bret would be a senior and Dana would be a senior's girl, going to all the upper-class parties. The year after would be rough, with Bret away at college somewhere in the Ivy League. They'd just have to bear up and wait for weekends, and write deliciously romantic letters.

Then she could either go to Bret's college, or one nearby. Someplace that had a good architecture department so she could pursue her career. After they both graduated, they could get married. She'd ask her sister, Maggie, and Faith and Shelley to be her bridesmaids. She wasn't sure whether they'd live in Boston, his hometown, or New York, hers. She knew she wanted two kids — a boy and a girl — but she and Bret would have to discuss that when the time came. It would be hard to manage both a family and a career as an architect, but Dana knew she could do it, as long as Bret was there in her life.

Dana hadn't mentioned any of these plans to Bret. Or to anybody else. But she just knew they'd come true because she and Bret were so right for each other. Nothing was going to change that. For sure not a few days of missed calls.

Besides, it *was* the week before finals, and Bret's study method was to let things slide all term, then cram like crazy at the end. So he was probably just off burning the midnight oil.

*   *   *

Dana was having a dream about Bret saving her from a burning building. Slowly she realized that the burning was her shoulders and the backs of her legs. And the hand on her arm wasn't Bret's, but Casey Flint's, gently shaking her.

"Hi," Dana said, waking up. Casey was a close friend of all three girls in room 407 Baker, and Dana was happy to see her now. "Is it lunchtime?" she asked her.

"No," Casey said. "I just cut study hall. I heard you were up here, and I didn't want it to be like in *Jane Eyre,* where her little friend gets sick one night and then before Jane knows it, the poor thing's deader than a doornail."

"Boy, are you cheery company," Dana said, propping herself against the pillows so that she was nearly sitting. "So nice of you to stop by."

"How're you feeling?" Casey asked, real concern showing in her eyes. Her flippant manner was just a thin layer on the surface of a deep, caring person.

"A lot better."

"Good, good," Casey said, but she was looking out the window next to Dana's bed as she said it. She sounded as though her mind were off somewhere else.

"Is anything wrong?" Dana asked her. Just because she was laid up with a sunburn didn't mean the whole world had stopped turning.

Maybe Casey was in some trouble. Maybe she was worried about something in her own life. Even though she was down herself, Dana wanted to be a good friend, to be *there* for Casey if she needed her.

But Casey denied that there was any problem.

"N-no," she stammered. "N-nothing's the matter. Nothing at all."

Chattering nervously was *not* Casey Flint's style, and so Dana pressured her a little.

"Case, I know something's wrong. It's written all over you. Please tell me. I'm your friend."

"I know that," Casey nodded, but looked at the floor as she spoke, as if she didn't want to meet Dana's eyes. "Dana. If you knew something that would hurt somebody you love, would you tell that person?"

"I don't know," Dana said. "I guess it would depend. Would the person find out anyway?"

"I think so," Casey said, choosing her words slowly. "Sooner or later."

"Could the person do something about the problem if she knew?" Dana probed further.

"Maybe," Casey said.

Dana added up all these factors and gave Casey her best advice: "I think you ought to tell."

When Casey didn't respond to this, Dana asked, "Who is the person? Maybe you could just tell me that and I could help you."

There was another long pause before Casey finally said, in a whisper, "You."

Dana couldn't believe her ears. "Me! *I'm* the one you know something about? Something that would hurt me?"

Casey just nodded. Dana sat there for a long time, crumpling the sheet on top of her in her fists. Finally she said, "It's about Bret, isn't it?"

Casey nodded.

"He was over at the tennis courts yesterday while I was playing. Just hanging out, sitting on the lawn, watching me and Julie West rally. I didn't know what he was doing there until we were through and he asked if I wanted some company walking back to Baker. I thought, why not, I like Bret, we're all friends. But then on the way — well, I'll skip the gruesome details — but he asked if I wanted to go to the movies with him Friday night."

"What'd you say?" Dana asked.

"Come *on*," Casey said, giving Dana an are-you-serious look. "I'll pretend you didn't ask that."

"Sorry," Dana said, staring down at the blanket, not able to look directly at Casey. "Why would he do something so dumb as ask one of my best friends out, though? Why wouldn't he ask somebody I didn't know so well?"

"I think he's already asked most of them," Casey said.

Dana was overcome with a mixture of hurt and disbelief.

"Well, of course, that's an exaggeration," Casey rushed in, seeing the misery in Dana's eyes. "But he has kind of been getting around lately."

"With whom?" Dana said with venom in her voice, as if she were going to put every one of these girls under arrest.

"What does it matter? Why get mad at *them*? They don't know what kind of arrangement you two are supposed to have. *Bret* does, though. He's the one you have to confront on this."

Casey stopped for a minute, then gave Dana a light tap on the arm with a knuckle, the most affectionate gesture her tough girl image would allow. "I didn't want to be the one to bring you this stuff, but I thought it was better than letting you sit around, thinking that he was being faithful and true. I just didn't want you to be a chump."

Dana reached out and put a hand on Casey's shoulder, and told her, "I understand. And it *was* the right thing to do — telling me. I just wish I didn't have to hear it, that it wasn't true. Do you think there could be a reasonable explanation — that maybe he was just kidding around with you and you misunderstood?"

"No," Casey said firmly. "I'm sure I got the message he was sending."

"But, Casey!" Dana wailed. "How *could* he?"

"I told you — that's a question you've got to ask *him*."

"I know," Dana said with resignation.

"And Dana . . ."

"Yes?"

"Whatever he has to say, it's better to hear it. Not knowing is like being an ostrich, sticking your head in the sand so you won't see what you're afraid of. That's a coward's way — and you're no coward. Here, I brought you a present." She dropped a pocket Pisces horoscope book onto the bed. "Your sign, right?"

"Yes," Dana said.

"See what the stars have to say about this," Casey said. "I have to get to class or Patrice Allardyce, headmistress with heart of ice, will toss me in her dungeon."

Dana opened the book to the entry for that day and read: "Trouble with member of opposite sex. Trust broken. Insist on meeting. Try for resolution. Good day for buying car or acquiring media publicity."

Dana closed the book. She didn't think she needed any media publicity and she didn't think she could get much of a car with the thirty-seven dollars she had in her savings account back home. So the only astrologically guided action she could reasonably take was to call Bret and find out what was going on.

He'll probably have a perfectly logical explanation that will have us laughing and hugging within ten minutes, she thought. She really thought she believed this, until she felt the tears streaming down her cheeks.

CHAPTER THREE

Dana called Bret that night, right after she was let out of the infirmary. As soon as she heard his voice on the other end of the line, she was instantly relieved. He sounded happy to talk to her, mad that nobody had told him about her sunburn. She sighed with happiness. It was the same old Bret she knew and loved. Everything was going to be all right.

"So," Dana said, "you want to see me before I peel?" Although she considered herself a feminist, she was still shy about asking him for dates. Usually, what she did was something like this, not asking him so much as making it impossible for him not to ask her.

"Sure," he said and laughed. "What's tomorrow — Friday? Yeah, I'm free if you are."

As much as she was sure everything was okay, Dana felt a fast-sinking stone of doubt drop into the pool of her heart. *Just how free*

would you be, Bret Harper, if Casey had said
she would go to the show with you?

And then, as if he had heard her thought,
Bret asked, "You want to go to the movies, or
what?"

"Why don't we just take a walk? Maybe
over to Ketchum Falls. I love these nights up
here. There's nothing like them back in New
York. Besides, I want to talk to you." She
tried not to make this sound too heavy. If he
picked up anything ominous in her tone, he
didn't let on.

"Great," he said. "I'll read two books at
once and sleep with another under my pillow
tonight so I'll be all studied up and ready to
play tomorrow."

She hung up feeling one hundred percent
better about everything.

The next night, half an hour before Bret
was supposed to arrive, Dana put on a double
coat of the aloe lotion Nurse Zinger had given
her. When she got to hard-to-reach spots on
her back, she asked Faith to help. Faith took
the bottle and pretended to read from the
label.

"Let's see. Hmmm. Interesting stuff. In-
gredients. Aloe. Extract of toad. Deadly night-
shade. Poison sumac syrup. Cobra venom.
Boy, you won't find this stuff at the Rexall."

Then Dana pulled on her loosest draw-
string pants and her lightest cotton shirt. She

was still so tender that everything she put on felt like a sandpaper straitjacket.

At seven, she ran downstairs and out onto the front lawn of Baker House. She sat on one of the stone benches and waited. At ten after, Bret came bounding up.

He always looked great. Even on his worst days, even the time he'd had the flu and his nose had gone all red and puffy, he was still in Oakley Prep's Top Ten. But sometimes he looked better than great, closer to wonderful. Sometimes his black hair was all feathery, his eyes dancing with light, his smile full of more teeth than other people's. Tonight was one of those nights.

Dana wished she could say the same of herself. If they were going to wind up having a romantic scene out at the falls tonight, she wished she could look a little more glamorous for it. But she suspected that being half red-and-shiny, half brown-and-flaky, tonight was probably not the night she was going to get hauled off to Hollywood for a screen test. Then she thought, *Well, maybe it's not quite that bad.* This thought lasted until Bret got a good look at her.

"Oh, honey," he said, sounding truly concerned, "I think they let you out of the infirmary too soon."

They walked through the campus, then down the road past Oakley Prep, and headed out in the opposite direction from Greenleaf, toward the falls. Bret did most of the talking. First, about a couple of courses he was worried about passing.

"The thing about trigonometry," he said, "is that it's not easy to learn all of it in the last three nights of the term."

Then about his roommate, Harvey Brewster III.

"The thing about rich guys is that they had maids all the time until they got here and they think *you* might as well be their maid now. They're slobs without even trying. They think the room is a giant wastebasket — that whatever they throw around will eventually get picked up. By elves or something. Anyway, O'Shea, our housefather, came in the other day and said we were Board of Health material, and gave us both citations. So, because of Brewster the Slob, I've got to go up before Dorm Board next week."

If he was worried about talking with her, or troubled about their relationship, he wasn't showing it. By the time they got to the falls and found a big flat rock to sit on and watch the moonlight play on the rushing water — a big romantic deal with Canby-Oakley couples — Dana was convinced that Casey must have been mistaken. She decided to get this stupid business out of the way so she could enjoy the rest of the night with him.

"You'll never guess what Casey thought the

other day when you wanted her to come with us tonight."

At the name "Casey," Bret jerked back a little and slipped his hand free of Dana's.

"What?" he said now, calm, but sounding careful, as if he suspected Dana was laying a trap for him.

"She thought that when you asked her to go to the show tonight, you meant *alone*, not with *us*."

"Oh," he said. If he thought this was a good joke, he was doing his laughing on the inside.

"Well, that *is* what you meant, isn't it?" She was giving him every opportunity to get out of this.

"I didn't know you'd want to get together tonight," he said.

"You mean you *were* asking her for a date, is that what you're saying?"

"I guess," he said, his voice dead.

"Bret. What's happening? I mean, aren't we supposed to be going together?"

He was quiet for so long that Dana began to think he just wasn't going to respond at all.

When he finally did, he said, "I guess I'm just not any good at this, honey." He turned toward her and took her hand in his. "I know I should've talked with you about it. Sometimes I'm just a coward. I knew you'd find out sooner or later, but I suppose I thought this way I wouldn't have to tell you. I'd just get caught. I'm sorry."

Dana pulled her hand away from his.

"Dana, I told you in the beginning that I wasn't a one-girl guy. I'm only seventeen. I think I'm just too young to get tied down yet. Plus, this fall I'll be a senior. I'd like more freedom. You know, it'll be my last year here and I'd like to cut loose a little."

She couldn't believe what she was hearing. Bret was throwing over their whole relationship so he could be a Big Man on Campus next fall. Could this possibly be the same person she loved and trusted so much? It couldn't. It was like some stranger had crept into Bret's body, like the pods in *The Invasion of the Body Snatchers*.

"So what happens now?" she asked the pod.

"I don't know. I guess that's up to you. I'd like to see you, but I don't know if you want to see me anymore."

"You mean we should still see each other, but be free to date other people once in a while?" Maybe she had overreacted. Maybe all he was saying was that they should loosen up on each other a little bit. She could handle that, as long as they knew it was each other they really loved.

"Well, not exactly," Bret said, bursting this small bubble of hope. He spoke slowly, as if he were carefully measuring his words before letting them out. "I was thinking about something more the other way around — that we should probably start dating other people, but still see each other once in a while."

"Keep in touch. For old time's sake," Dana said. Bret didn't catch the sarcasm in her voice.

"Something like that. I don't want you to disappear on me. You've been such an important person in my life this past year."

"I'm not dead yet," Dana said, her hurt turning to anger. "You can stop sounding like you're speaking at my funeral."

"Sorry."

Dana looked across the stream. On the opposite bank, she could see another couple in the moonlight. They were holding hands and talking low and nuzzling each other like young colts. Then the guy pulled something out of his pocket and slipped it onto the girl's finger. A going-steady ring, probably. Dana sat in the silence between her and Bret and thought about this other couple, just starting out on their romance as hers was ending forever.

At this, her tears gushed like the falls they were watching. For some reason, it was much worse that Bret wanted to stay friendly with her. She'd rather think he couldn't handle seeing her around, that it would tear him up to run into her when she was with her new boyfriend. (What new boyfriend?)

She couldn't run very far with this fantasy. Bret wouldn't care if he saw her with another guy. He wasn't saying all these things to be cruel. He had simply stopped loving her — at least in the way she wanted him to. But why? When? How could she not have noticed? She had a hundred questions about this. But she couldn't ask any of them. She knew that his answers would only make her feel worse. Better to get out with at least a few shreds of dignity.

And so, on their walk back to Baker — a walk that usually seemed way too short, but tonight seemed to go on forever — Dana tried to steer the conversation away from what had just happened at the falls, toward "safe" subjects.

"Are you still going to take the dance intensive this summer?" She tried to make it sound like light interest, but secretly she wanted to know if she was going to have to be running into him all the time for the next month. It would be so much easier if he'd just go home to Boston.

"Yeah," he said. "I'm staying." He spoke reluctantly, as if Dana were prying the information out of him. It was as if now that they had decided to break up, he wanted her to disappear. But then, after they had walked a while in silence, he seemed to change his mind, probably realizing that silence was more awkward than whatever fake talking they could do.

"Yeah," he went on. "I figure it's a nice artsy thing I can do to rattle my proper

Bostonian dad a little. He wants me to be an investments analyst and maybe I will, but first I want to kick up my heels a little."

Yeah, Dana thought bitterly, *in more ways than just dancing.*

What she said, though, was, "Well, if you're going to kick up your heels, you might as well take dancing and learn how to do it right."

He smiled his great smile, just the way he always had when they had been in love. He always had said Dana had the most terrific sense of humor. It seemed as if he still thought so. It was so hard, walking along with him like this, joking around like they always did, to believe that they weren't still together, that he didn't still love her like before. She could hardly bear this knowledge, but she knew she had to put up a brave front or else she would collapse completely and embarrass herself.

"Yeah," she said, although he hadn't asked her anything. She was just desperate to keep the conversation rolling. "I'm really looking forward to the poetry intensive. I figure it's going to take all my energies for the next month."

Who am I kidding? she asked herself. *Do I really think he'll believe this for a second?*

"I thought of that," Bret said. "It's good you're going to be busy for a while."

Why, you conceited creep, Dana thought, but she couldn't think of a retort to the remark. He knew she was going to be hurting and so did she.

"But I can hardly even think about the intensive yet. Right now I'm just so excited to get down to New York. My mom has tickets for us for a really good ballet and a play that everyone's raving about!" She tried to sound as bright and carefree as she could. But her only wish at the moment was to get through the front doors of Baker without breaking down or doing something foolish. She almost made it.

That is, she made it as far as the steps of Baker House. A sentimental place for them. They had kissed good-night here a hundred times. And here they were kissing now. But tonight he was kissing her on the cheek — the kind of kiss you give your Aunt Edna to thank her for the pajamas she gave you for Christmas.

The kiss was also different in another way. This kiss wasn't good-night — it was good-bye.

Suddenly Dana couldn't stand it, couldn't bear to just turn and walk up those steps, away from the first boy she ever really loved.

"Oh, Bret!" she threw her arms around him. "Couldn't we try just a little longer? I thought you wanted us to last forever."

"Things change," he muttered. "People change." He gently pulled himself out of her embrace.

"But couldn't we stay together just for the

summer intensive. Just one more month? To make sure this is what you *really* want?"

"Dana. This *is* what I really want. I'm not going to change my mind. I'm sorry."

He didn't wait for her to say anything else. He just turned and walked away and then, when he got to the sidewalk, broke into a run. Dana stood there, watching him go, now feeling humiliated on top of hurt. She didn't go inside; she couldn't face anyone right now. She just sat down on the steps and stayed there two hours, until curfew.

Alison came out to shoo away the last of the dates and lock the front door. She was already almost back inside when she spotted Dana. She came down and put a hand on her shoulder. Dana didn't move.

"You okay?" she said with real concern in her voice.

"No," Dana said.

"Why did I even ask? I hate asking stupid questions. Of course you're not okay. Come on in. I'd let you sit out here all night, but I can't."

Dana followed her up the steps, but once inside didn't wait while Alison locked up, as she ordinarily would. She just kept walking toward the stairs like a zombie. Soon she heard the slapping sounds of bare feet running on the marble floor.

"Hey," Alison said, grabbing Dana by her elbow, "stop, will you? Just for a minute."

Dana stopped, but didn't turn around. She couldn't face Alison just now.

"How about coming up to my penthouse for a tea nightcap?" Alison offered. "I'll pour the tea and you can pour your heart out."

Dana shook her head.

"Too soon?" Alison asked.

Dana nodded.

"It's all bottled up and it seems too scary to let the cap off just yet?" Alison prompted.

Dana nodded, with her back still to Alison.

"Just answer me this. Is it about Bret?"

Dana turned. She didn't say anything. She didn't have to. The tears pouring down her face were her answer to Alison's question.

CHAPTER FOUR

W ait," Faith said to Shelley, who was behind her going through the cafeteria line. "Here's a riddle. What's gray and wet, with brown stuff floating in it?"

"I give up," Shelley said.

"Whatever it is, they're trying to pass it off as dinner tonight." Faith pointed at a large pan set into the steam table.

"Chipped beef," Shelley said with certainty.

"How can you be so sure?"

"Look. They're serving toast with it. If there's toast, the murky stuff is chipped beef. If there's rice, it's chop suey. If there's noodles, it's spaghetti sauce. If there's potatoes, it's stew. I've cracked the code."

They both took a pass on the chipped beef and moved down the line.

"What're we going to do about Dana?" Shelley asked.

"How many days has she been in bed now — two or three?" Faith asked.

"Today's the third. She got up yesterday to go to her Spanish final, then came right back. Today she just skipped her philosophy exam entirely. She says no philosophy of life can make any sense of what Bret did to her, and so why bother with it." Shelley mused for a moment. "How long do you think she can live on chips and orange pop?"

"Oh," Faith shrugged. "I'm not so worried about that. I think scientists are on the brink of discovering that chips and soda are the world's most nutritious foods. No, it's not Dana's peeling, skinny bod that worries me, it's her head. I've never seen her like this — nowhere even near this. I may get weird and you may get funky, but Dana's always been Miss Even Keel."

"But she hadn't been dropped by Bret then — not just dropped, pushed out of the plane without a parachute. I wish she could see that Bret Harper's not the only fish in the lake."

"Sea," Faith corrected. "It's 'only fish in the *sea*.'"

"Lake's the same thing."

"It isn't. You're always just missing an expression. Or jumbling it up. Like the other day you said something was spilt milk under the bridge. It makes my ears go nuts."

"Okay, okay," Shelley said. "I wish Dana

would see that there are other ducks in the pond."

"You're impossible. Now what do you suppose *this* is? You're so smart about main dishes, maybe you can identify this USO — unidentified sitting object. From the fact that it's sitting at the end of the line, I'm thinking it might be something in the dessert family. Molten lava pudding, maybe."

Shelley peered at the tiny bowls filled with a viscous substance. She looked like a fortune-teller reading tea leaves.

"Apple brown betty" was her identification. "Don't take it" was her judgment. "Have an apple. My rule of thumb here is try to take the stuff they haven't been able to mess around with."

Once through the line, they looked for and found an empty table. As they were taking their plates and silver off their trays, Casey cruised by on her way out of the cafeteria. She stopped to talk with them.

"Do I look lumpy?" she asked them.

"Why?" Shelley said. "Are you gaining weight?"

"Just the weight of a peanut butter and jelly sandwich and an apple. I'm smuggling. I'm going to try to coax Dana into eating something with a little substance."

"She won't listen to us about that," Faith said. "Won't talk to us either. She's pretty much shut us out since the big night. I'm glad to hear she's letting you in a little."

"I think it's kind of by default," Casey said. "I think she's embarrassed around you two. You both have boyfriends — two, in your case, Shel. I think that just adds to her humiliation. I'm more in her boat. No guy on the horizon. And then, with all my family problems this year, I guess she sort of sees me as a troubled soul. And so it's all right to be troubled around me."

"Oh, but I wish she *would* let it bleed on us a little," Faith said. "We're her roommates and we love her. And it's hard being around her when she's so stony silent. It's hard to know what to do."

"Just let her be for a little while longer," Casey said. "Nobody I know ever died of a broken heart. Or even kept on with one for very long. She'll get through this."

When she got to room 407, Casey didn't bother knocking on the door. She didn't want to risk being told to go away.

"*Dinnah* is served!" she said, making a whooshing entrance, flourishing the sandwich and apple.

"Not hungry," Dana said and rolled over on her bed so that her back was to Casey.

"If that's a hint," Casey said. "I'm not taking it. If you won't eat, you'll just have to go on an empty stomach."

No response from Dana.

"Why, go where, Casey?" Casey said to herself, then answered her own question.

"Why, to the amusement park at Crystal Lake, of course."

At this Dana not only rolled back over, but propped herself up on an elbow.

"Crystal Lake?" she said. "Amusement park? Roller coasters and cotton candy when I'm feeling like this? You have *got* to be kidding."

"I'm not," Casey persisted in the face of this considerable lack of enthusiasm. "I know something about depression. I've been there a couple of times myself. The one thing the depressed brain most wants to do is lie around and think about how depressed it is. The only thing to do is beat it at its own game. Show it who's boss. Take it to Crystal Lake and make it have fun."

"It won't work on me," Dana said, running spread fingers through her long brown hair.

"How can you know if you won't try?"

More silence from Dana.

"The other thing is that some of the girls are beginning to talk about you. Word's getting out that you've been holed up here for three days. Pretty soon someone's going to tell someone else, who will tell some guy at Oakley, who will tell Bret. I don't know about you, but I wouldn't want the guy who shot me down to have the satisfaction of thinking I was still flat on the ground."

Dana sat all the way up when she heard this. She looked hard at Casey, then looked hard at the wall, thinking this through. Finally, she said, "Give me five minutes to brush my hair and put on some jeans."

The amusement park's name was Funland, but everyone just called it Crystal Lake, which is where it was. It was much more famous than the lake itself, which was small and rocky-bottomed and not used much except for fishing.

The park was open from May through October. Dana had been there a few weeks before. With Bret, of course. And so she was not particularly eager to go back and open the wound of bittersweet memories. On the other hand, Casey was probably right. A lot of kids from Canby Hall and Oakley Prep went over to the park on warm nights like this one, and her appearance there, laughing and having a good time, would almost surely get back to Bret.

As they walked through the gates — gaudily painted plaster pillars in the shape of clowns — Dana was surprised to find her spirits lifting a little. For the first time in three days, the tight knot in the center of her chest seemed to loosen a bit.

This probably *was* a good place for a depressed person, Dana thought. Everything was so brightly colored. Calliope music poured from the merry-go-round. Screams of delicious fear drifted down off the roller coaster. Everywhere she turned, some gravel-voiced person with a portable loudspeaker was trying to lure them onto a ride or over to a booth where they could toss rings over pegs or baseballs or bowling pins, and win prizes.

"So," Casey said in a cheery voice that matched their surroundings, "where to? Which ride should we try first?"

Dana looked around. She and Bret had gone on practically every one of the rides, hugging each other tightly through the fake terrors. Getting on any of them now would only bring those wonderful moments washing back over her.

"Is there a bed ride?" Dana asked Casey. "You know, where you just curl up and the ride doesn't do anything, just lets you turn over and stare at the wall and be by yourself."

"That is not the spirit we're looking for here," Casey said firmly and took Dana by the arm. "*I'll* do the selecting here." She looked around. "Okay, here we go. Onward to the merry-go-round!"

Fortunately, the merry-go-round was one of the few rides Dana and Bret had skipped. It was just too babyish. So Dana let Casey buy them a couple of tickets and lead her by the hand onto the circular menagerie.

"Pick your animal," she directed Dana.

"I don't care."

"Well, then, get on this duck," she said and gave Dana a push up into the saddle, then hoisted herself up onto the tiger next to it. The ride started up almost immediately, going round and round, faster and faster, the tiger and duck rising and falling in time to the calliope playing the "Blue Danube Waltz."

"Hey!" Casey yelled over to Dana. "How's it going there on old Donald?"

Dana had to crack a smile — her first, she realized, in three days.

"See?" Casey said. "I told you. It's a well-known psychological theory that it's impossible for a person to remain depressed while sitting on a duck."

After that, they went on the Bumper Cars, then the Tilt-a-Whirl, then the Wild Mouse, and the Round-Up. By that time, they were hoarse from screaming, and ravenously hungry.

"Nothing like being scared out of your wits to make you really work up an appetite," Dana said.

"You must be feeling better if you're thinking of food."

"I am. Thanks, Case. I would've never thought something as dumb as coming out here could help lift my mood, but I think it has."

They got a corn dog, a piece of pizza, a puff of cotton candy, a bag of caramel corn, and a couple of large Cokes. They brought this picnic over to one of the tables in the clearing next to the midway, and sat down to eat it and watch the passing parade of funsters.

"You want to talk about it?" Casey asked Dana as she passed her the cotton candy.

"Well, it's the only blue food I've ever eaten."

"Not about the cotton candy, dope. You know what I mean. I thought it might do you some good to get it off your chest a little."

Dana was silent for a long moment before saying anything.

"It changes," she finally said. "At first, I was just so hurt, I couldn't really think. Then I got mad. First at Bret. You know — how could he do this to me? Then I got mad at myself. For not seeing it coming. And then embarrassed. I'm afraid I was not too cool at the end. At the last minute there, I sort of turned to mush."

"You didn't fling yourself on the ground before him and kiss his hand and tell him you'd kill yourself if he didn't stay?"

Dana surprised herself by laughing.

"Close. I'd been doing well all the way back from the falls. I told him it had been fun, no hard feelings, no regrets. I wished him a happy life. I was so cool. And then when we got to the door I just sort of crumpled."

"Give me details," Casey said.

"I can't. It's too embarrassing."

"Please. Then I can see if it's really as bad as you suspect."

And so Dana gave Casey every gory detail.

"That's not so bad," Casey said when she was finished. "Girls tell me worse than that every day of the week." Casey was confidante to half the girls at Canby Hall, it seemed, and so Dana thought she probably *had* heard some pretty grim tales.

"Tell me worse, then," Dana prompted. "You don't have to name names."

Casey thought for a moment, nibbling caramel corn and staring off into the middle distance.

"Okay," she said. "Last week a certain Ms. X told me that when a certain Mr. Y and she broke up, he told her to get out and stay out of his life, he never wanted to see her again, to please just leave him alone forever and for a while after that, if possible. And then she walked back to her dorm and called him up and asked him if he'd like to go to the movies the next night."

Dana whistled. "Hooo boy. That *is* pretty bad. I think I'm feeling a little better. I mean, I'm not out of the woods, but the trees *are* beginning to shrink from redwoods to oaks."

CHAPTER FIVE

"To guys," Dana's mother toasted. "The dear rats." And clinked her glass of white wine against Dana's ginger ale. Dana had wanted orange soda, but her mother overruled.

"I think you'd give the waiter heart failure," she said.

They were having dinner at Naples, a fancy Italian restaurant in Manhattan, near the apartment where Dana's mother and her sister, Maggie, lived. Dana's father had lived there, too, before the divorce.

This dinner was supposed to be a celebration of the end of Dana's first year away at school, and her brief homecoming. She was going back up to Massachusetts on Sunday to begin the summer intensive.

Ordinarily, Dana would love celebrating like this. She loved eating out in restaurants. Even cheap restaurants like El Burrito, which was her favorite. But tonight she was de-

41

pressed again about Bret. These blue feelings about him went away for a few days at a time now, then sneaked up behind and ambushed her when she least expected them. Plus she expected this dinner was not so much a celebration as a consolation prize. To make her feel better about Bret. She also had a sneaking suspicion — since Maggie had begged off on some flimsy excuse — that her mother was getting her alone for a Big Talk.

Dana looked across the table. Her mother looked especially great tonight. A side effect of her job as department store fashion buyer was that she was a terrific dresser. Tonight she looked incredibly chic in a dove gray silk shirt and skirt, with a rough cotton shawl in deep purple thrown over her shoulders. And for a flashy touch, she was wearing drop earrings made of tiny, multicolored beads.

Dana thought for a minute. Her mother had dated in high school and college and then been married and now was divorced and beginning to date again. She probably had a lot of valuable experience in all this and — given the toast she had just made — clearly wanted to share some of it with Dana.

But Dana wasn't sure she wanted to get into the subject. It made her nervous. Sitting in a fancy restaurant, chatting with her mother about boys and men, love and heartbreak. It seemed like one of those modern things characters in movies did, not real people in real life.

She was saved by the waiter, who arrived just after Dana's mother's toast. He wanted to tell them about the specials. The list was so long that by the time he got to the end, Dana had forgotten what was at the beginning.

"Gee," she said. "I hope there's not going to be a quiz on this."

"It's okay," he said and smiled. "I've got a cheat sheet for you." He handed her a card with the specials printed on it.

Dana noticed then that he was kind of cute. She was amazed that she *did* notice. She hadn't looked at a guy with any interest since her breakup with Bret.

When the waiter had gone, Dana studied the card, then the larger menu, and tried to make some choices.

"I think," she said when she was done, "I think I'll have a bowl of minestrone and the marlin."

"Do you know what marlin is?" her mother asked.

"No."

"It's a fish. Sort of like swordfish."

"Good. I just liked the sound of it. Eating in the cafeteria at Canby Hall gives you a philosophical attitude about food. You give up having to know exactly what it is that's on your plate."

Her mother laughed, then grew serious. "You really like it up there, though, don't you?"

"Oh, *yes*. Or at least I did until I got wiped out by my boyfriend last week. Since then I feel like I'm looking at the world through mud-colored glasses."

"I . . . ," her mother hesitated before going on, "I wanted to talk with you about that."

"Oh, Mom. I'm not sure I can talk to you about Bret. Not just yet anyway."

"Oh, *Bret*," her mother said, dismissing him with a fluttery wave of her hand. "I'm not really very concerned about him. He's just the first in a long line-up."

"I wish I had your optimism," Dana said wistfully.

Her mother got a really serious look on her face. She knitted her brows and leaned forward. All this was a sure sign that she was about to be sarcastic and completely outrageous.

"Well, to tell you the truth, we *have* been worried, Maggie and I. We even called your father this week to get his opinion on the plan."

"The *plan*," Dana repeated. There was no stopping her mother once she got on a roll like this. The only thing to do was play along until she got to the punch line.

"Yes. A last hope for you. When we heard that it was off between you and Bret, we figured you'd never get another boyfriend.

Our hopes for marrying you off were dashed.
So instead, we're apprenticing you to a family
of goatherds in Albania."

"Oh, Mom, you're terrific," Dana said, taking her mother's hand in heavy mock gratitude. "You knew I wanted a career in the
outdoors."

And then the waiter was back to take their
order. Dana took another look at him. He
was cute. For an older guy. He looked about
thirty. Still, that didn't mean she couldn't
smile back at him after he looked up from
writing down her order and smiled at *her*.

Her mother took in this exchange of eye
contact and, when he had gone, said, "Oh,
yes, you'll be without a boyfriend for some
time. Maybe as long as seventy-two hours.
Which is my point — that boyfriends aren't
the point."

"I guess I know that," Dana said and
sighed. "I'm just not sure what *is*."

"You. You're the point. Boyfriends are
great. Well, some will be greater than others.
And endings will usually be a lot less fun
than beginnings. But you can't count on boys
or relationships to make you happy or confi-
dent. That has to come from inside *you*. If
you hitch your good feelings about yourself
to other people — to having a boyfriend, or
being popular — then you're a cork on the
cruel seas."

"I do feel pretty corky these days," Dana
said.

"The thing is, honey, you went up to Canby Hall last fall and whoosh! — you got hooked up with Bret right off, and then floated over a lot of the rough spots. You never really had to be on your own in a new place. You never really got to flex and test your strengths. I think this summer might be your second chance — to find out what being independent is like."

"Well," Dana said, "I sure managed to be boyfriendless for all the time before Bret came along."

"That's right," her mother said, remembering. "How did you handle it so well then?"

"I just lied to everybody. I said you wouldn't let me date yet. And then I cried up in my room on Saturday nights."

"Not true."

"Sometimes true," Dana answered, then got stuck, then found the words. "You know, Mom. About Bret."

"Yes?"

"I really loved him. It wasn't just fun and security and all that. It was really love." With this, she started to cry, trying to hide her tears.

"I know," her mother said, taking her hand. "I know it's all raw inside you. I guess all you can do is think about the Stones."

"Huh?" Dana said.

" 'You Can't Always Get What You Want,' " her mother said.

Dana couldn't help smiling, even in the middle of her tears. She felt like one of those freak storms where it rains while the sun is still shining.

"Here's the thing that's driving me nuts, if you want to know the truth," Dana said. Now that she'd started talking there was no stopping her. She couldn't even remember why she'd been scared to start in the first place. "I'm really looking forward to the intensive. Getting to work with Grace Phaeton — I can hardly believe it! But I've got this nightmare fantasy about Bret."

"Running into him when he's with a new girl?" her mother said.

"No, it's much stupider than that. It's that I go into someone's dorm room and there's Bret's picture, tacked up on *her* bulletin board. And I have to sit there and try to act normal while I'm really sick inside."

Her mother thought a moment, then said, "Well, I don't know if this is much help, but I can tell you that in my whole life, not one of the really sickening scenarios I feared *ever* happened."

"Well," Dana said. "That *is* good to know."

"It's the sickening stuff that you *don't* imagine that comes true!"

"That's the thing I love about you," Dana said as the waiter approached with their dinner. "You're so reassuring."

"Well, what are mothers *for*?"

CHAPTER SIX

Dear Sarah,
    Hey, big sister, where were you last night when I called home? I talked to Mom and Richard, but you were out with *Eric*. Now, who might *he* be? You're not telling your little sister everything.

I was going to come home during this break between the end of the regular school year and the beginning of the summer intensives, but it's only a week and Washington's a long haul from here and I've got too much to get done.

I want to beef up my portfolio before the photo intensive starts. The guy who's teaching it has a whole book of photos published. Called *Night Cities*. He went around the country and took photos of what people were doing at night — just walking around, having block parties, sitting in the movies, waiting in emergency rooms. Some of it's pretty heavy stuff. Anyway, I don't want to walk in there next week with my box of pictures of Alison's kitten. I was thinking of doing something like *Greenleaf at Night*; then I remembered that there is no Greenleaf at night (ha ha).

Things are still wonderful with Johnny. In addition to being adorable (well, he *is*), he is also the first boy I can really *talk* to. I wish he'd lived next door to us all my life. I miss not having had him around for all the years before this one.

Dana's not so lucky in love. Bret dumped her. Dropped her flat so she wouldn't cramp his style. He wants to be a Big Romeo on Campus. Poor Dana's walking around looking like her soul got run over by a truck. She's down in New York now for the break. It'll probably do her good to see her mother and sister and go shopping and see some ballet, which she loves. At least it'll get her mind off Bret for a few days.

Well, Shelley just came in with a big crisis here. She's in the middle of polishing her nails and needs someone to do the right hand. You can see that being a roommate is a lot of heavy responsibility and commitment.

Sisterly love (in spite of the fact you aren't telling me about your new boyfriend),

Faith

CHAPTER SEVEN

The room was completely dark. The lights were off. The shades were pulled, the cracks sealed off with black tape. The desks had been pushed aside and the eleven students in the poetry intensive were lying on the floor, flat on their backs, breathing shallowly.

The only sound was Grace Phaeton's voice, lowered almost to a whisper.

"Now all your senses are deprived," she was saying. "Here in the darkness and silence, you will be free to turn toward your inner selves and find the poetry within. You'll be able to listen to the voices of your souls."

Dana just got the shivers and chills when Grace Phaeton said stuff like this. Apparently, though, not everyone in the poetry intensive shared her rapture. In the middle of the silence that followed Grace's words, someone in the darkness croaked, "Ribbit," indicating to everyone else that the voice of his soul was froggish.

In a flash, the lights went on. Dana's heart jumped at the sudden change in atmospheric conditions. Hurricane Grace was bearing down upon them.

"*Who?*" she said, exhaling the word, like the caterpillar in *Alice in Wonderland*.

Sheepishly, Ronald Stillwell grinned and said, "It was me. Froggy."

Ronald was not the brightest guy at Oakley Prep, but it was rumored he was the richest. His parents were in Nepal on a Himalayan trek. They had dropped him into the intensive to keep him busy until they got back. He wasn't very happy about the situation. He thought poetry was "more boring than watching paint dry" and let everybody know it.

"What I'd really like to do this summer," he had told a bunch of the kids after the first day of the intensive, "is a comic-reading, TV-watching, pizza-ordering intensive. An independent study. At home while my folks are away."

It looked like he was going to get his wish. Grace Phaeton, who was very tall and imposing with her swept-up, salt-and-pepper hair and hawklike features, loomed over Ronald as he sat on the floor. She glared down at him with a look like the one the wicked witch gave Snow White just before she put her to sleep.

"You may leave now," she said, unfurling an arm within the voluminous blouse she was wearing and pointing to the classroom door.

"Leave," Ronald repeated after her, as if

he were a soldier in drill. "Do you mean just for now, or did you have something more permanent in mind?"

"Mr. . . ."

"Stillwell. Ronald."

"Mr. Ronald. I'm not sure how many more years I've left to me in life, but however many, I hope you will be so kind as not to show up in my presence during any of them."

"B-b-but-t-t," Ronald stammered, "what am I supposed to do? Can I stay up here? My folks aren't even in the country. I can't really go home."

"Well, I don't know, Mr. Ronald. I'd suggest you go to Las Vegas. I'm told it's a haven for bad comics. You might pursue your career to some advantage there."

A fairly amazing feature of Grace Phaeton was that she didn't seem to realize that her students were teenagers. Or she didn't make a distinction between teenagers and adults. Or she didn't think the distinction was important. She was often astonished that they hadn't spent a few years in Europe ("on the Continent" was how she put it) or seen a lot of great ballet in New York. And right now, she was probably at least semi-sincere in her career advice to Ronald.

And so there was nothing he could do but throw his knapsack over his shoulder and trudge out of the room. When he was almost to the door, he turned and vaguely threatened Grace Phaeton.

"My folks aren't going to like this," he muttered.

"Oh, but I'm sure they'll forgive you when you make a success of yourself in show business," she said, and then was back to reestablishing the mood that had been so rudely destroyed.

"Ah, my flowers of the night," she said, "I will return you to the darkness you love," and flicked off the switch.

"And then she just threw him out," Dana told Shelley and her boyfriend Tom, who had been passing by as Dana came out of the intensive. They were on their way into town to shop for jeans for Tom.

"His parents will be the ones who do the real croaking when they find out," Shelley said. "His family's been tied up with Oakley for a jillion years. One of the dorms is even Stillwell House."

"I don't think Grace Phaeton knows any of that," Dana said. "And she probably wouldn't care about it if she did. I wish you guys could've been there when old Ronald slunk out of that classroom. I'll bet it's the first time in his life anyone's told him off."

"So you're liking the poetry thing?" Tom asked.

"Oh, *yeah*," Dana said. "Phaeton's the greatest. And I feel so *immersed* in poetry. It helps me keep my mind off, well, off other things."

"The only poem I know," Tom said, "is 'Poems are made by fools like me. But only God could make a tree.' "

"Trees are next," Dana said. "Nature. Our assignment for next time is to sit alone out in the wilderness and commune with nature and use the inspiration to write. But the poem doesn't have to be *about* nature. If we listen to crickets and it makes us feel like writing about taxicabs, that's okay."

"But if a taxi goes by, can you write about a cricket?" Tom teased her.

"You just don't have a poetic soul, Tom."

"I just might, Dana. I just might. I think I'll write a poem and give it to you and you show it to Grace Whatsername and we'll see what she says. How about that?"

"I want to see this poem first," Dana said.

"Well, I don't think I'll make it about a taxi. The only one around here is that beat-up Plymouth Ed Hodges drives. I might write about the fuzzy dice he has hanging from his rearview mirror. They're kind of poetic."

"Great," Dana said. "Well, I hate to leave you two, but this is where I cut out. I have to go change my clothes and then I'm off to the wilderness. At least to the ridge off Old Fort Road. I figure that's about as wildernessy as I feel like today. I'm pretty easily inspired. I don't need rain forests or mountain lions."

"Well," Shelley said. "Be careful. Don't talk to strangers."

"Oh, Shel, I think a stranger is just what I need about now."

When Dana had walked off a ways, Shelley told Tom, "She's still sad most of the time, but I've got a feeling she's beginning to get over Bret."

This was true. Dana was still hurt and confused about what had happened with Bret. But she had managed to push it to the back of her mind. The sad thoughts now mostly came up only when she was alone. During the Intensive days and when she was with her friends, she felt much better.

Of course, I haven't seen him yet. That'll be the big test, she thought, walking down the path toward Baker. Suddenly she stopped, blinked hard, and rubbed her eyes in disbelief. *This is ridiculous*, she thought. *You don't just think about seeing someone and then — poof! — there he is, like magic. This is impossible!*

But sure enough, there he was, living and breathing and heading straight for her on the path. By the time Dana finally gave in and admitted that he wasn't a figment of her imagination, it was way too late to pretend she didn't see him and veer off in another direction.

The worst part was that he wasn't alone. He was half of a couple. The other half was Renée Rivette, a French exchange student at

Canby Hall. Before they spotted Dana, they were the perfect picture of the Young Couple in Love. He was holding her hand, she was holding a small bouquet of just-picked wildflowers. Both of them were doing so much smiling at each other, they looked like they were in a smiling contest.

Renée was petite, with long black hair and dark eyes. Not only was she beautiful, but she had this adorable little accent that dropped boys in their tracks. It was probably inevitable that she and Bret would find each other — it was like nitro finding glycerin. Actually, when Dana had tried to imagine whom Bret would move on to, Renée was up there near the top of the list.

But thinking about Bret and Renée as a possible item and seeing them together in the flesh were two different things entirely. Dana simply couldn't stand it.

First, her knees felt like they were going to buckle underneath her. Then her heart started pounding like a huge mallet inside her chest. Then she felt her face get nearly as hot as when she'd had her sunburn.

Her emotions were a jumble of rage, jealousy, longing, love, hate, and despair. And yet, with all this going on inside her, she knew she had to somehow manage to work her face into a smile and try to look casual. She concentrated and pulled her lips back until she figured it probably looked pretty much like a real smile.

"Hi, Bret," she said. "Hi, Renée."

Renée's response to this was to ever-so-casually drape her arm over Bret's shoulder. At this, every jealousy light on Dana's board lit up. She felt an almost irresistible impulse to leap over and pry that arm off his shoulder. How dare she cozy up to Bret like that?

Then, in a flash, Dana realized that Bret was not only not her boyfriend anymore, but he was someone else's. Now it was Renée who drifted off to sleep at night in her dorm bed on a cloud of Bret thoughts.

This drove Dana from nervousness into nausea. She felt like someone was doing a Dutch clog dance inside her stomach.

"So," Bret said, sounding like Mr. Casual, "how've you been?"

"Oh, great," Dana lied. "Real busy. How's the dance intensive going? Casey thinks it's rough."

Dana had been talking to Bret, but Renée stepped in to answer the question.

"Oh, eez *formidable* — how do you say? — terrific! We dance all zee day and zen Bret and I, we dance all zee evenings, too." She paused and smiled up at him, then turned back to Dana. "You know — zee practice."

At this, Bret began to look a little uncomfortable.

"Yeah," he said, clearly trying to pull the talk back to some neutral plane. "Neither of us is a natural, and so we've got to really work at it. I'll tell you, my feet have never been so sore."

At this, Renée began to giggle and tug at the short sleeve of Bret's T-shirt.

"Tell her about zee day you keeked your foot into zee wall."

Bret looked down at Renée and gave her sleek hair a playful tousle, then smiled and shrugged at Dana.

"Baryshnikov I ain't," he said.

Dana could see that on one level, this was a perfectly normal conversation. But at the same time, she knew that if she had to stand here one minute longer, witnessing these two lovebirds cooing at each other, she would probably go insane. And so she said, in what she hoped was a bright, cheery tone of voice, "Well, I have to get going now. Between the intensive and my social life this summer, I'm on the run all the time." She didn't think she'd get away with this lie, but as soon as she'd said it, she could see displeasure flicker behind Bret's eyes. Jealousy? Maybe he really believed that she was going out with half a dozen gorgeous guys. Well, let him.

"It was nice running into you," he said now, back in control, his voice smooth as a disc jockey's. "Keep in touch."

As Dana walked away, the only kind of touch she could imagine between her and Bret Harper was a nice, swift sock to his jaw.

CHAPTER EIGHT

Dana — in shorts and running shoes, her long brown hair streaking out behind her as she ran like the wind, her feet pounding against the hard-packed earth of Old Ford Road — was heading for the ridge.

Dana had loved running ever since she started a couple of years back. Lately, it had been one of her biggest helps in getting past thoughts of Bret. Country music was the other help.

Until the breakup, country songs had seemed silly to her. Now, though, the lyrics seemed to have been written expressly for her. Before, "heartache" was just some vague, meaningless concept. Now she understood it all too well. Now she knew how loving someone who didn't love you back could give you an actual pain deep inside your chest.

Whenever the pain hit, she found her running shoes and Walkman, put them on, and shot out of Baker House and out across the

Canby Hall campus. Some days she ran into Greenleaf. Some days she ran through it and beyond, into the green, rolling, Massachusetts hills. Today, though, she was headed in the opposite direction — out to the wildflower ridge she had discovered this spring.

The ridge was her "thinking spot." Whenever she needed an alone place to work through heavy thoughts, Dana sat up there — by herself, looking down on the campus, feeling far enough away from her life to get a little perspective on it.

Today, though, she was not going up there to think. Nor was she going to brood about Bret.

"Argh," Dana said to herself, since no one else was around. Then she pushed the "hold" button on all thoughts about Bret Harper. This afternoon she couldn't be spacing. She had to focus all her energies on the assignment ahead.

She had picked the ridge as her place to try communing with nature. When she came out of the small woods and ran to the crest of the ridge and looked down over the purple and pink sea of wildflowers, she knew that if nature were ever going to speak to her, it would be here.

She took off her Walkman. She suspected Grace Phaeton did not have in mind a four-way communion between Dana and nature and Crystal Gayle and Merle Haggard.

She slipped off her backpack and got out her lined spiral notebook and a felt-tip pen. She sat down and waited for inspiration to strike.

What arrived instead was a fat yellow bee, buzzing around her feet. Dana leaped up and ran around in a circle a few times, glad that no one was around to witness this idiocy.

When she had gotten rid of the bee, she sat back down and this time closed her eyes to try to capture nature through her other senses. Grace Phaeton said the poem didn't have to be about what they saw. It could be about how nature smelled or sounded or felt on their skin.

For a few minutes, the only sounds Dana heard were the wind rustling the wildflowers, a few crazily happy-sounding birds, and a fly. Then there was an under-sound, like the bass reverberating on her stereo. The sound grew louder and louder until it was drowning out all the other noises of nature. It was the sound of a fast-approaching horse.

Dana opened her eyes to see the horse — a creamy palomino, galloping toward her full-tilt. She jumped up faster than she had for the bee. The horse came to a dust-exploding halt just a few feet in front of her. It wasn't until then that she looked up and noticed its rider. He was beautiful. Handsome was not the right word. He was beautiful. His hair was blond and longer than the guys at Oakley wore theirs. It curled in locks of pale gold around the collar of his chambray workshirt.

His face was narrow with a thin nose and high cheekbones. His eyes were a steely gray. Right now they were looking down at her coldly.

"Whatcha doin'?" he asked.

"Communing with nature," she said, trying to be cute, then realizing in an instant that this guy would not see the cuteness. This guy was probably thinking she was an idiot. He just kept looking straight at her. He didn't seem in any hurry to speak.

When he finally did, he said, "What's communing?"

Dana was getting really sorry she had started this.

"I'm supposed to write a poem for class. About nature. I'm sitting here waiting for an inspiration to strike. I'm getting in touch with the nature around here. You know — communing."

"Oh," he said.

A big talker, Dana thought.

What seemed like five minutes later he said, "I guess I'll have to charge you a communing tax then."

"Huh?" Dana said, then thought, *Boy, I'm about as sparkling a conversationalist as he is.*

"You're communing on my family's land."

"Oh!" Dana said and picked up her backpack, as if he had said she was sitting on his family's chair.

"It's okay," he said, taking off the bandanna tied around his neck and wiping his face with it. The day had come up warm and sunny and he looked like he had been riding hard. The horse was shiny and breathing heavily. He looked around at the vast panorama of field and woods. "I guess there's room for you to stay here awhile. If a bear comes along, though, you might have to give up your place." He smiled a slow smile.

It was an incredible smile. Dana felt like a big, soft net had been dropped over her. She was unable to move, but also unable to say anything very clever. Anything at all, really.

"Name's Randy Crowell," he finally offered.

A Crowell, Dana thought. The Crowells were one of the big landowning families around Greenleaf.

"Dana Morrison," she managed to say.

"You go to the girls' school, I suppose?"

"Uh-huh," she said, looking up at him, using her hand as a visor over her eyes. With the sun behind him, he was hard to see. And hard to talk to, sitting up there on his high horse. But she tried.

"You go to school in Greenleaf?"

"Nope."

When it became clear that he was not just pausing in midsentence, but had stopped speaking, Dana burst out laughing.

"Well, don't rush in with too much information about yourself," she said, surprised at herself. "Who knows, I might be a detective."

He smiled that incredible smile again.

"I graduated a week back. I'm only seventeen, but I started early. Skipped kindergarten. I was much smarter when I was five."

"You going to college in the fall?" she asked.

"Nope. Staying right here. We've got a big apple orchard and we breed horses for a lot of the stables around these parts. There's a lot of work to be done, and I'm real needed. Besides," he said, and then dropped in one of his Grand Canyon pauses, "I love it here. No place else I'd rather be. Where're you from? Not around these parts."

"No. New York."

"We've got some of my mother's kin in New York. Up in Hunter's Junction."

"Oh, I meant New York City. Manhattan."

"Yep. I've heard of that, too. It's south of Hunter's Junction, I believe." There was a twinkle in his eye that tipped off Dana to the fact that her leg was being pulled.

Suddenly, he pulled his horse's head up by the reins. It had been chewing on the wildflowers.

"Got to be going," he said. "Stay as long as you like. Anybody comes to run you off, it's just one of my brothers throwing his weight around. Tell him I said you could stay."

"Thanks," Dana said. And then, as if she were the heroine in a cowboy movie, she watched the beautiful blond guy gallop off on his horse.

Before he had gone very far, though, he turned the horse around and came back.

"Be all right if I gave you a call some-time?" he said.

"Sure. Yeah," Dana said, trying to sound casual, as if it were every day she made dates with guys who rode into her life on horse-back.

He started to turn the horse around again to leave.

"Don't you want a number?" she asked.

He looked over his shoulder just before cantering off.

"That's okay. It's not too hard usually to find a girl — if a fella really wants to."

And then he really did ride off.

Dana sat back down amid the wildflowers and tried to get back to the business of com-muning. But it was no use. After an hour, she gave up.

CHAPTER
NINE

Shelley's clock radio came on with the news that this was going to be the hottest June day in Greenleaf's history. It was supposed to push into the upper nineties. Even at seven, it was already muggy in 407 Baker.

"*Upper nineties*," Shelley repeated after the announcer, in disbelief.

"I already feel like a lizard on a rock," Faith said from her bed, running a hand through her short, shiny curls, pulling the hair back off her face. "I've been awake since five, just lying here, trying to get the energy to get up. It was hot at *five*."

"It doesn't seem so bad to me," Dana said, stretching her way out of sleep. "But then, I just love summer."

"What happened to the old Heartbreak Kid?" Faith said. "It sure seems to me that in the last couple of days, we've had a big attitude change. Ever since she spent the afternoon out on the ridge."

Dana just looked back innocently. She wasn't talking. Faith and Shelley knew something was up, and were insanely curious, but no amount of teasing or prying had gotten Dana to reveal anything more than a lot of mysterious Mona Lisa smiles.

"How are we ever going to get through intensives today?" Shelley asked, sitting up in bed. Her bangs were stuck to her forehead, damp with sweat just from the effort of sleeping. "A few days ago, Rosofsky had us do imitations of pieces of bacon frying. Today I could do that without even trying. But I don't know if I could do much of anything else."

When they got down to the cafeteria, in search of as many icy glasses of orange juice as they could get away with, they found a CLASSES CANCELED ON ACCOUNT OF HEAT notice posted at the door.

"Oooooh," Dana said. "A free day! Let's all go swimming!"

"Oooooh, let's!" Shelley and Faith squealed in tandem, imitating Dana's untypical enthusiasm. But this sarcasm was lost on her, and so they let it go. Besides, spending a day this hot out at Hudson's Creek was not a bad idea at all.

They made some calls and rustled up Casey Flint, and Faith's boyfriend, Johnny Bates. Shelley's friend Tom had to work, and Bret was not on the guest list. The four girls and Johnny were ready to go by ten o'clock.

They walked out Old Fort Road, past Dana's ridge. She gazed at it intently as they passed, looking for a fast palomino, but she didn't see anything.

Hudson's Creek was the best swimming spot around. The water was bright blue and cool, with deep and shallow places and a big flat rock in the center for tanning. Further down, there was a thick rope hanging from a branch of one of the trees. The rope had a big knot at the end, and if you were brave, you could stand on the knot, hold on to the rope, and let a couple of other kids pull you back and launch you out over the creek. When you got to the middle, you let go.

The sides of the creek were sloping, grassy banks, perfect for drying off and lying around and drinking Cokes and flirting. The social scene at the creek was extremely active. It was a popular meeting place for Canby girls, Oakley boys, and kids from Greenleaf High — so popular that the town council had hired a lifeguard to sit out there to make sure no one drowned while trying to impress someone else with the backstroke.

Even at ten-thirty in the morning, when the five of them got there, the creek was packed.

"Standing room only," Johnny said. "They look like water-packed sardines."

"I think I see a free patch of grass way down there on this bank," Shelley said, peering through the rhinestone-studded harlequin sunglasses she had picked up at a flea market as a lark.

They made a run for it, leaping over tanning bodies, dodging around trees like forty-niners in the gold rush, and staked their claim with five beach blankets and a small red-and-white-striped beach umbrella of Dana's. Johnny had brought a six-pack of soda and a piece of rope, which he now tied through the plastic piece that joined the cans. He dunked the cans into the cool creek and put the other end of the rope under a rock to secure it.

"Nature's refrigerator," he told the girls. "It's the most useful piece of information I got out of two years in Eagle Scouts."

They all sat there on the spread blankets for about thirty seconds before Shelley said, "I can't stand it even one micro-millisecond longer. If I don't get into that cool water this instant, I'll die! Come on everybody — last one in's a rotten egg!"

"A *fried* egg," Faith said, running after Shelley,

"Poached," yelled Johnny, following them down to the water.

"Boiled," said Casey.

"Benedict!" shouted Dana, bringing up the rear.

They all stopped and turned around and said in unison, "Benedict?"

"Sure," Dana said. "Eggs Benedict. They're poached on English muffins and covered with hollandaise. You get them at brunch in New York restaurants."

"Throw her in," Casey commanded. "Around here, all snobs get dunked."

"Oh, no!" Dana screamed, seeing what was coming, and tried to run, but there was no place to go fast enough with all the kids lying around. And so she got caught right away. Her four captors brought her down to the water's edge, then sat her in a human slingshot made up of their linked hands and arms. They proceeded to give her the old heave-ho.

"One . . . two . . . three!"

And in she went. The others quickly followed — running, jumping, diving. They dunked each other and chased each other and took turns on the rope swing and played chickenfight and just generally let the water change them from sixteen-year-olds into ten-year-olds.

After they had swum themselves out and dried off in the sun and eaten all the chips and drunk all the soda they'd brought, they lay back on their blankets. Faith, Shelley, and Johnny fell asleep. Dana stayed under her umbrella — she wasn't about to get *another* sunburn — and talked with Casey.

"I'm so glad I decided to stay for the summer session. It's neat, isn't it — being up here now?"

"Yeah," Casey said. "It's fun being able to

wear shorts to class and not *having* class until ten in the morning. It's more like camp than school."

"Except better," Dana said. "There's no bugle at dawn."

They laughed, and Casey looked over at Dana and said, "You sure seem happier than you did a week ago. Is there something you're not telling old Casey?"

"Mmmhmm," Dana said, nodding.

"Something you're *going* to tell old Casey?"

"Maybe. I'm not being coy. I just want to wait on this one a little. Right now, it's in the category of Something That Might Happen. If it slides over into Something That's Happening, you'll be the first to know."

"Fair enough. Just tell me this. Has this mysterious possibility erased Bret Harper from your mind?"

"It's helping. So is time. I'm off the critical list now, just among the walking wounded. That is, I can manage not to think about him most of the time, but when I see him out on campus, holding hands with Renée, or whoever, I feel like someone threw a medicine ball at my stomach."

"I think you have to expect that," said Casey in her Ann Landers, Confidante-to-Millions tone of voice.

"Yeah?" Dana said, eager for whatever words of wisdom Casey had on the subject.

"Oh, yeah. When Suzanne Robbins got

dumped by Larry Townsend last winter, it was a month before she could see him without throwing up."

Casey said this with a straight face. She was offering it as a serious piece of information, but the vision of Suzanne Robbins throwing up every time she saw Larry Townsend hit Dana squarely in her solar plexus of humor.

"Did she . . . ," Dana started, then had to stop because she was laughing too hard, "did she have to carry those little airplane-sickness bags around with her?"

At this, Casey caught the laughing bug from Dana, and the two of them were so loud that they woke up the three nappers.

"Hey," Johnny said. "What's going on here? Didn't you two read the DO NOT DISTURB sign I hung on my nose?" Then he said to Shelley and Faith, "I think these two giggling maniacs need to be *cooooled* out a little. What do you think?"

Dana and Casey didn't wait for the verdict. As long as they were going to get thrown into the drink, they figured they might as well jump in on their own. And so they were off at a run, with the other three close behind.

"What time is it?" Shelley asked Faith as they neared the Canby Hall campus at the end of their long, slow walk back from the Creek.

Faith looked at her watch. "Just past four."

"Oh, then I'm okay. I told Tom I'd meet him at Pizza Pete at five. He wants to treat me to a pizza — an offer I'm not about to turn down, especially since I saw that creamed cod is tonight's delicacy in el cafeterioso."

As they approached Baker House, Shelley said, to no one in particular, "Gee, that guy over there looks familiar."

"Who?" Dana asked.

"Leaning against the pillar on the front steps. Oh, my goodness! It's Paul!"

"*Your* Paul?" Dana said. "Iowa Paul?"

"It must be a mirage," Shelley said, blinking, as if that would change what she was seeing.

"Mirages are ponds," Faith interjected. "Not people."

"But what can he be doing here?" Shelley said.

"I think you're about to find out," Casey said, nodding toward him with her head. "Because he's just seen you, Shel, and he doesn't look like he thinks *you're* a mirage."

And sure enough, Shelley looked up to see Paul waving with excitement, then starting into a slow run toward them. When he got to Shelley, he picked her up in his arms and whirled her around. Once. Twice.

"Oh, Shelley," he said, as if nobody else were around. "It's so good to see you. Are you surprised?"

"Oh," Shelley said as he put her back down

on the sidewalk. 'I don't think *surprised* is a strong enough word. What *are* you doing here? At first I thought you had to be a mirage."

"Nope," Paul said, pinching his arm. "I think this is the real me. I've known for a couple of weeks that I'd be coming out this way to look at a couple of colleges, but I thought I'd just leave that information out of my letters and phone calls so I could have the pleasure of seeing your jaw drop to the ground."

"Which I'm sure it did," Shelley said, laughing.

"Just about."

"Now," he said, backing off. "Are these the infamous girls of 407 Baker?"

"Oh," Shelley said, seeing that everyone was just standing around, not knowing how to fit into this reunion. She introduced them to Paul, and as she did, she noticed that he seemed taller, and somehow older than the last time she had seen him. He looked really sharp today — black jeans and a black polo shirt, setting off the tan he had gotten working on Al Benson's farm, which he did every summer. His brown hair was blond at the ends — bleached out from the Iowa sun. She felt so proud of him. After all she had told Dana and Faith about him, she wanted him to live up to the picture she had painted. And he really did.

Now he was kidding around with Faith and Johnny. He seemed to get along with everyone so easily. Maybe they should go into town together for dinner. Get a pizza or something.

Pizza! How could she have forgotten? She took Dana's wrist and lifted it so she could see her watch. It was nearly four-thirty. She was supposed to meet Tom in Greenleaf in half an hour! What was she going to do? She needed help. She looked at her friends, wondering whom she could recruit. Not Dana. She was still too bruised from Bret to drag her into this mess. Not Faith. She had her own boyfriend already here and wouldn't fit into the scheme that was taking shape in Shelley's mind. That left Casey.

"Oh, Paul," Shelley said, squeezing his hand. "Let me go upstairs and take a quick shower. Your surprise was great, but you caught me at a pretty grubby moment. I want to look as nice for you as I can. Especially after all this time."

"Sure," he said, giving her a fast hug. "I'll just wait down here. I haven't really had much of a chance to walk around the campus."

"Good," she said, and then putting an arm around Casey, said, "Can you come up with me, Case? I'd like to borrow that red blouse of yours."

Casey gave her a *What red blouse?* look,

but was cool enough not to say anything. When they were out of Paul's earshot, Shelley said, "Oh, Casey, will you help me?"

"I gather this is in reference to the Two Boyfriends Dilemma?"

"Yes. But I've got a plan. It's a little risky, but if there's anyone who can pull it off, it's you. Now just listen carefully. . . ."

CHAPTER TEN

"So what do you think about my plan?" Shelley shouted over the noise of rushing water to Casey in the next shower stall.

"I think it sounds like a bad episode of *Three's Company*," Casey shouted back.

When they were out of the showers, drying off, combing their hair, Casey went on.

"Plus," she said, "I don't think we'll get away with it. As great an actress as you are and as intrepid a troublemaker as I am, I just don't think we're going to be able to get through a whole pizza making Paul believe that Tom's *my* boyfriend and making Tom believe that Paul's just an old classmate of yours from Iowa. I mean, basically what you've got here is a stupid, sure-to-backfire scheme."

"But you'll do it with me?" Shelley asked.

"Of course," Casey said, smiling.

Ten minutes later, Shelley and Casey, in fresh jeans and T-shirts and splashes of

Casey's *Essence d'Amour* cologne, met Paul downstairs, out in front of Baker.

The walk into town was easy. No one had to pretend anything. If Paul thought it was a little odd that Shelley was bringing Casey along on their big romantic date after months of not seeing each other, he was too polite to say so. Shelley just told him that she and Casey and Casey's boyfriend had planned to have a pizza and he seemed to take it in stride.

When they got to Pizza Pete, Tom was already there, sipping a Coke in one of the back booths. Casey maneuvered it so that she'd be the first one to get to the booth. She slid in next to Tom and scruffed the top of his head to make fun of his short-short summer haircut. He was working part-time as a tour guide on the Greenleaf Garden Walk and the two women who ran the tour had insisted on his getting "the clean-cut look." The girls had been teasing him about the cut for a week now, so it probably didn't seem too odd to him that Casey jumped in next to him to tease him a little more.

Introductions were trickier. Casey and Shelley fairly tripped over each other trying to keep both guys in the dark.

"Hey, Tombo," Casey said, using an affectionate nickname she had just made up. "This here's Paul — all the way from Shelley's hometown in Iowa. He's scouting schools out this way and so we thought we'd show him what kind of pizza they serve in New England. It could make the crucial difference in whether he decides to come East for college next year."

Then Shelley leaped in, hoping that Paul had interpreted Casey's friendly tousling of Tom's hair as a gesture of affection between girlfriend and boyfriend.

"Tom lives here in Greenleaf," she told Paul, "and is a lifelong expert in regional junk food."

The two guys shook hands across the table. So far, so good.

"You still in high school?" Paul asked Tom.

"I'll be a senior next fall. Here at Greenleaf High."

"Then you'll go to college around here afterward?" Paul asked.

"That depends on a lot of things. My grades. My dad's money. Shelley." At this, he smiled across the table, his eyes locked lovingly on his girlfriend.

"Oh, yeah," Casey jumped in. "Shelley's sent away for one of those guides to colleges. We're all waiting until it gets here to see what these schools have to offer. It's so confusing trying to decide." As she was saying this, Casey casually put her arm up on the back of the booth, so it would look as if she had it draped across Tom's shoulders, but just high enough that he couldn't feel it. She thought this was a stroke of particular brilliance.

"I didn't hear anything about this book," Tom said, not cooperating with the scheme. "I'm impressed. You girls must be serious — already thinking about college when you're barely finished with sophomore year."

"Well, Canby Hall's a pretty high-pressure school," Shelley injected hurriedly, trying to move things along rapidly so that Paul couldn't stop to dwell on why she was a factor in Tom's choice of college.

"Are you and Shelley *old* friends?" Tom asked Paul innocently.

The hurt showed in Paul's eyes. Clearly he was wondering why Shelley hadn't mentioned him to this friend of hers. He looked at Shelley and said, "I can't remember exactly, sweetheart, can you? I suppose we go back to first grade."

Fortunately, the waitress picked this particular moment to arrive at their table with menus and glasses of water, and created enough of a diversion to allow Casey to tell Tom in a low voice, "It embarrasses Shel like crazy, but what's she going to do? I guess she got picked Pine Bluff Corn Sweetheart a few summers back and everyone back there has called her sweetheart ever since."

To Shelley's relief, they spent the next five minutes deciding what size pizza they wanted, and what to get on it. For five blissful minutes she didn't have to be trembling with the fear of discovery. She glanced across at

Casey, who gave her a conspiratorial wink. Great. To Casey, this was clearly just a game. To Shelley, it was a horror show.

How had she let herself get into this mess? Why hadn't she just told Paul she had to go to a meeting with her drama coach, then run into Greenleaf, had this stupid pizza with Tom, then begged off with a headache on account of the heat, and run back to campus for a romantic moonlight walk with Paul? A great, *easy* plan. Why hadn't she thought of *it* instead of this absolutely insane stunt she was in the middle of now? This wasn't the first time Shelley felt she had a knack for passing by the logical, easy solution for the difficult and incredibly stupid one. *Well, no sense crying over spilt milk under the bridge,* she thought with a sigh. Now that she was in this far, she had no choice but to go through with it.

And deep in her heart, Shelley knew the problem was not in her choice of schemes, but in getting herself into a situation that *required* schemes. Her problem was not having a pizza with her two boyfriends, it was having two boyfriends in the first place, and keeping them a secret from each other.

An interesting thing was that Paul and Tom seemed to be really hitting it off. When Shelley tuned back in to the conversation, they were talking baseball, and they had gotten into a lively but clearly good-natured argument.

Shelley thought this would probably be a good opportunity to duck out for a fast strategy update with Casey.

"I'm going to go to the ladies' room. Want to come with me?" she said to Casey.

"No," Casey said, "I'll just stay here."

One swift, under-the-table kick in the shins and Casey said, "On second thought, I think I *will* come with you."

Luckily, no one else was in the bathroom, so they could talk freely.

"So," Shelley said eagerly, "how do you think it's going?"

"Pretty well," Casey said. "It's fancy footwork, but I think we're doing great."

"I don't think they have a clue, do you?" Shelley asked hopefully.

Casey was giving her short blond hair a fast brushing in front of the mirror.

"No," she said dismissively. "Hey, they're *guys*. When it comes to romance, boys are thicker than Bombay elms. Dense, my dear, really dense. It's what gives us girls such an advantage in matters of the heart. Come on. Let's go back out."

"But what'll we do?" Shelley asked, getting nervous all over again.

"Just keep on doing what we've *been* doing. Come on. It'll be a breeze."

"But," Shelley said, tailing Casey out of the bathroom, "what am I going to do when we leave here? Who am I going to go back with?"

Casey didn't answer. As it turned out, her answer wouldn't have mattered anyway. When they got to the booth, there was no Paul, no Tom, just a note written on a folded-over napkin in the center of the table.

On the outside was printed in capital letters written with a ballpoint:

> FOR TWO GIRLS WHO AREN'T
> AS SMART AS THEY THINK

Inside was the message:

> SEE YOU AROUND.

It was signed:

> TWO GUYS WHO AREN'T AS
> DUMB AS YOU THINK

CHAPTER ELEVEN

They had a talk," Casey said, standing next to the table, rereading the note. "How could we be so dumb as to leave them alone with each other? We should have figured that they'd start talking and put two and two together and come up with four." She slapped her palm on her forehead to show Shelley what a knucklehead she felt like.

"Yeah," Shelley whimpered. "And you thought *they* were thicker than Bombay elms. How thick does that make *us*?"

"Where do you think they went?" Casey wondered aloud, turning the note over, as if half-expecting to find a secret message about the boys' whereabouts.

"What does it matter?" Shelley wailed. "If they're sitting outside on the sidewalk, or on a boat to Rangoon, it's all the same. Wherever they are, they're out there hating me."

Casey nodded. She had to admit this was probably true. She searched around in her head for something cheerful to say to Shelley in this definitely uncheerful moment.

"Well, you can always look on the bright side," she said.

"What bright side?" Shelley asked, trying to pull her tears back into sniffles in case there *was* a bright side.

Casey looked over Shelley's shoulder at the waitress approaching them. As she set a large aluminum pan on the table between them, Casey said, "Well, we got the whole pizza to ourselves!"

At this, Shelley burst into tears.

Of course Shelley couldn't eat a bite of the pizza, or even think of dinner back at Baker. Faith and Dana didn't even try to talk her into coming down to the cafeteria with them.

"Nobody as miserable as you are," Faith said, "is in any shape to face the Baker House dining room. It could be suicidal."

Shelley tried to smile. She knew Faith was trying hard to cheer her up. But it was no use. Shelley was sunk too deep in the mess she'd made of her life. She felt as if she were being pulled down into quicksand.

While the other two were at dinner, Shelley sat motionless at her desk, hating herself. Not the way she used to hate herself back in Pine Bluff when she was younger. In those days she had hated herself mostly for what she thought she wāsn't — thin enough, clever enough, popular enough, pretty enough.

No, this was another kind of hating. A worse kind. Now she had gotten some confidence, lost some weight, made a lot of friends, attracted some boys. And what had she done with all this good luck? Behaved like a jerk.

She deserved to get caught, she thought. She was a two-timing creep and didn't deserve one boyfriend, let alone two. And now they were both gone.

Suddenly, her sadness started seeming highly tragic — like the lives of the heroines of the thick romantic novels she read. She wove a fantasy like this around herself.

She was unworthy of love, and so she would have to go off somewhere — alone. Missionary work seemed like a good solution. Laboring in the farthest reaches of the jungle, selflessly helping others in a lifetime of making up for having been such a conceited, thoughtless fool in her youth.

She saw herself in a white doctor's coat, her hair bleached out by the pulsing equatorial sun. With one hand she was putting a cold compress on the forehead of a feverish native patient; with the other, she was scratching behind the ears of her pet lioness cub.

"Shelley. Shelley!"

How could anyone be calling me wāy out here in the jungle? Shelley wondered, then realized she had been deep in fantasyland and that the voice was calling from reality-land.

"Earth to Shelley," the voice was saying. It belonged to Ruth Freid, who lived on the second floor of Baker. She was standing in the doorway to 407.

"I guess I was spacing," Shelley said, and smiled sheepishly.

"There's a guy downstairs looking for you," Ruth said.

"What's he look like?" Shelley asked. It could be either Tom or Paul.

"Tall. Blond. Sad."

Paul.

"Thanks, Ruth," she said. "I'll change and go right down." She tried to sound calm. She hardly knew Ruth and didn't want to spill her troubles and confusion and anxiety all over. Once Ruth was gone, though, Shelley rushed down the hall into the bathroom and turned on the cold water full blast in one of the sinks. She bent over and splashed the water on her face, to try to calm herself. She was anxious to go down and try to straighten things out, but also humiliated by her behavior that afternoon, and dreading the possibility of a horrible scene.

She dried off her face, went back to 407, and changed into a plain white polo shirt and jeans. Paul liked her best when she looked fresh-scrubbed, clean-cut country, and she wanted to please him tonight.

Dana came in while Shelley was putting on a splash of cologne.

"Gee," Dana commented, flopping onto her bed piled high with cotton-covered pillows. "You're sure all dressed up just for a night of sitting around being miserable. Do I detect the aura of returned boyfriend around here?"

"Dana," Shelley said, shaking her head in admiration. "Sometimes you are so amazingly perceptive. Paul *just* came back."

"I know. I saw him sitting down in the lobby." Dana smiled her sly imp smile. Shelley had to smile, too, in spite of her nervousness about going downstairs.

She told Dana the conclusion she had come to about what a completely rotten person she was.

"I'm going to devote the rest of my life to self-sacrifice to make up for it. I think I'm going to become a missionary."

"You can't."

"Why not, may I ask?" Shelley said indignantly.

"They have snakes in the jungle."

"Oh, they do, don't they?" Shelley said, the wind gone out of her sails. "I forgot."

"Shel," Dana said seriously, getting up off her bed, and coming over to where Shelley was standing. She put a hard hand on each of Shelley's shoulders and looked her straight in the eye. "You don't have to become a missionary to make up for being a terrible person, because you're *not* a terrible person.

You were in a dumb situation. It's dumb to be going steady with someone who's a thousand miles away. Starting to get interested in Tom, who is alive and well and living right here in Greenleaf, just makes sense. The only crummy thing you did was not tell either of them what the situation was. And even that's really more weak than horrible."

Shelley looked at Dana, started crying a little, simply out of gratitude for the kindness of her words, then gave her a hug.

"What would I do without you, Morrison?"

"You wouldn't have all my smelly running socks lying around the room," Dana said. "What are you going to say to Paul when you get down there? Have you thought about that?"

"I'm not sure," Shelley said pensively. "A lot depends on what he has to say. I'll just have to punt, I guess."

The lounge of Baker House, one of the oldest buildings on campus, was oak-paneled and populated with overstuffed sofas and armchairs and an Oriental rug. Paul was sitting on the edge of a chair when Shelley came down to meet him. He didn't see her at first. He was sitting forward, his elbows resting on his knees, his chin in his hands. He was clearly deep in thought.

Shelley stood for a moment just looking at him. She remembered when she loved looking at him more than anything in the world.

She thought there was no boy more handsome. Now she thought that, although he was good-looking for sure, his nose was probably a little on the big side, his chin a little weak. Realistically, he was probably closer to average than to Adonis. He looked up and saw her.

"Hi," he said very softly. She almost wasn't sure he had spoken.

"Hi," she said and sat down on the hassock in front of his easy chair. "You want to go outside — take a walk?"

"No. It's nice in here," he said and looked around. It *was* nice, with the big, leaded-glass windows thrown open to catch the summer night, the antique brass lamps turned low. "And I don't have much time. I'm supposed to show up at Harvard sometime tonight, and I don't want to be wandering around Massachusetts until two in the morning."

"I'm sorry for this mess," Shelley said, and really meant it. She wanted to say it up front. "I don't have any good excuses. I just let the whole situation snowball until I couldn't see a way out of it. And then you took me by surprise today and instead of facing the music, I just leaped into the first harebrained scheme I could think of."

"I don't think it even had the brains of a hare," he said disgustedly.

"It didn't, did it? How long did it take you guys to figure it out — about a minute?"

"About. It was pretty embarrassing — for both of us."

"I can imagine. I feel terrible."

"We got over it. We're both big boys."

"Where'd you go?"

"Over to his place. We watched the last half of the Red Sox game."

"I can't believe it! Here I am in torment, and he takes you home to watch baseball. That's Tom, though."

Suddenly Paul was looking at Shelley with very sad eyes.

"Do you love him?" he said. Now his eyes were beginning to gloss over with the beginnings of tears.

"I don't know," she said honestly. "I like him. We have a good time together. I haven't known him that long. I don't fall in love overnight."

"You did with me," he said and smiled with the memory. "Our first date. We went to see that movie about the haunted house and then we went to Daddyburger's and then we drove out to the bluff and we kissed. And later on you told me you'd fallen in love with me then and there."

"It's true," Shelley said, remembering the moment herself. "But I was only a child then. Now I'm sixteen and sophisticated and mature and I don't do things like that." She smiled to let him know she was kidding.

"The thing is," Paul said, taking her hand,

"I really think he's a great guy. I mean if *I* like him, that must say something."

"He *is* great, Paul. But so are you. This isn't a greatness contest or anything like that. I think the problem between you and me would still exist even if I hadn't met Tom. We're a thousand miles apart," she said, using Dana's line of reasoning. "Every day a hundred things happen to each of us that we can't share with each other. We were bound to drift apart a little. *And*, I suppose, to find people nearer to us to share things with."

"I know," Paul said, with a faraway look in his eyes. "I've begun to share a few things with someone else, too."

"*Who?*" Shelley shrieked, then caught herself and repeated softly, "Who?"

"Oh, Amanda Lewis."

"Oh," Shelley said, avoiding his eyes so he wouldn't see how upset she was.

"We're not dating yet. I just, well, I see her a lot around school. It's kind of a fate sort of thing. Our schedule cards must've got stuck together going through the computer. Anyway, we've got five out of six classes together. So I see her a lot around school. Sometimes I give her a ride home. She lives right out our way."

Shelley felt like a thermometer. With each fact about how cozy Paul was getting with Amanda Lewis, the mercury inside her rushed further toward the top. About two more facts and she'd explode.

"I like Amanda," Shelley said sweetly. "Did she ever get those braces off her teeth?"

"Shel," Paul said, looking disappointed in her. "Come on. You're not being fair. You not only want to have your cake and eat it too, but you don't want to let me have any cake at all."

She felt ashamed. He was right.

"I'm sorry," she said. "I'm trying to grow up. Some moments I just slip back a little. Other moments I slip way back. Right there I slipped back to about first grade. I didn't want to share my crayons with Amanda Lewis."

"You know," Paul said and smiled, "one of the best things about you is that you may be wrong, but you're always the first to admit it."

"I guess that's kind of grown-up, isn't it?" Shelley said, with hope in her voice.

"Sure. And you know, you're a lot more grown-up than when you left Pine Bluff — today's stunt excluded. So am I. We're both changing so much. It's kind of exciting."

"Sometimes it's a little too exciting," Shelley said. "Sometimes I get scared."

"Me too," Paul confessed.

"Big tough Paul Braddock — scared?" Shelley was amazed.

"Sure," he said, looking out the window at the softly rustling leaves of the huge oak tree outside. "Let's go for a walk, okay? I need to be alone with my old girl."

Shelley took him along the paths of the campus, through the park at the center, on into the birch grove, down the footpath into the maple grove. The maple grove was the quietest place around Canby Hall.

"Stand still a minute," she told him when they were in the middle of it. They stood there, not moving, breathing as shallowly as they could for a long moment. "See. You can't hear anything," she said. "Not even crickets. I guess they don't like maples, or something. This is where I come when I want to be really alone."

"Have you been here with Tom?" he asked.

"No," she said. It was the truth. She wished Paul had gotten angry with her about all of this. It would have been easier to deal with than his being so hurt by her dishonesty and by her feelings for Tom. "You're the first person I've ever brought here," she reassured him.

He looked at her a long time, as if trying to find the answers to a million questions in her eyes. And then he kissed her. When they pulled apart, he said, "We've still got something special, don't we?"

"Oh, yes," Shelley said, nodding at how much she still felt for him. It added to her confusion, but it made her feel better, too.

"But you also like Tom and I also like Amanda. Is this crazy?" Paul asked.

"I think it's probably normal crazy," Shelley said and laughed. "I think at our age, being normal crazy is about as sane as you can hope for," she said, feeling very wise.

"I guess. But can we do this without losing each other?"

"I don't know." Shelley shook her head. "I think we'll just have to let the future be a question mark. See how things go. What do you think?"

"Okay," Paul said. "If you're willing to give it a try, so am I."

They sealed the plan with a kiss, and by the time Paul drove off half an hour later, Shelley felt better about things than she had in quite some time.

All that remained was to straighten things out with Tom. Fired with confidence from her successful talk with Paul, Shelley went to the downstairs pay phone and dialed Tom's number.

His mother answered. She had seemed to like Shelley the times they had met, but her voice was noticeably cool and distant now.

When she came back on the line, she said, "He says he'll talk to you later."

"Oh," Shelley said. "He's busy?"

"No. He's just up in his room sorting his socks. I think he wants time to figure out what he wants to do."

Shelley was so embarrassed. Not only wouldn't Tom talk to her, but he'd told his mother all about it, no doubt in terms that were not particularly flattering to Shelley.

She barely made it through ā polite set of good-byes before hanging up.

She came back into the room, and Dana looked up from the poem she was working on. "Shel, what happened? If it weren't nine o'clock at night, I'd say you got a sunburn while on that phone."

CHAPTER TWELVE

Dear Mom,
   I'm writing this under hardship circumstances. Sometimes I wonder how I get anything done living in this mini-insane-asylum known as 407 Baker. I'll try to paint you a picture of what's going on here at this particular moment (although almost any other moment would probably be just as nuts).

Faith is in the process of pinning up about a hundred photos of a leaf. It's the same leaf in every photo. The point, she tells us, will become clear when all the photos are up. She says if we scan them left to right, top to bottom, like reading the page of a book, we'll see the leaf move in the breeze.

This is a project for her photo class. She'll have to put it up again in her classroom, but she wants to try it out on us first. Now, you have to understand that there's no way Faith could do this much pinning up and taking

97

down in silence. Heavy work like this *must* be accompanied by Michael Jackson played at nearly full volume on her portable stereo.

Shelley has earplugs on so she can concentrate. What she's concentrating on is being "The Wind." This is today's assignment from André Rosofsky, her acting coach. About every five minutes or so, she blows through here with a dozen scarves tied around her neck and waist and arms and legs. When she gets out the door, or to her bed, or to the window, she crumples into a little heap and lies there looking like a dead, multicolored Kleenex until the next breeze kicks up.

About two minutes ago, The Wind ran out the door and smack into Casey, who's practicing leaps in the hall for her dance intensive.

In the middle of all this, I am just trying to write a simple letter to you. But it ain't easy.

The poetry workshops are wonderful. I'm enclosing a couple of my poems. They're nowhere near as good as Grace Phaeton's, of course. (Did you read her book yet? I left it by your bed.) But I'm leaps and bounds ahead of where I was at the beginning of the summer.

There's progress in other areas, too. I can now see Bret around campus, even when he's with another girl, and *not* feel like I suddenly have a 104-degree temperature.

And I've met someone new who seems interesting. This is TOP SECRET. I haven't even told the RMs (roommates) or Casey. His name's Randy Crowell and I met him three days ago. His family owns a farm around here. He said he'd come looking for me and I think he will. He just doesn't seem like the kind of guy who'd hand a girl a line. He's the absolute opposite of Bret, from what I can tell.

Do you care if I date a country boy? What am I asking *you* for? You're the one who sent me up here to the sticks. Here's the consequences.

Oh, can you get me a couple more polo shirts? It's so hot up here that I'm running through them faster than I can get down to the laundry.

Bunches of hugs to Maggie.

Your darling daughter,
Dana

CHAPTER THIRTEEN

When Dana was done with the letter, she threw her green nylon backpack over her shoulder and bounded down the four flights of stairs from her room. She was on her way into Greenleaf for a BSM — Basic Supplies Mission. She needed a stamp for the letter, a bottle of hair conditioner, a couple of cans of chunky chicken for late-night hunger madness, and new batteries for her Walkman.

Two things hit her as she pulled open the heavy wood front door of Baker House and emerged from the relatively cool lobby out into the summer midafternoon. The first thing to hit her was a blast of heat that was like opening an oven. The second thing was Randy Crowell, who was loping up the front walk, heading straight for her.

The double effect of these two surprises was like having the wind knocked out of her.

When she and Randy were face to face,

Dana said, in a voice so low she could barely hear it herself, "Hi."

Brilliant, she thought. *Here I go again, impressing this guy to death with my wit and wisdom.*

"I was just looking for you," he said, taking off his straw cowboy hat and wiping the sweat from his forehead with the tanned back of his hand. "I didn't expect it to be quite this easy."

"Well," Dana said, "I got a telepathic message that you were coming, and so I ran down here to meet you."

"No kidding," he said.

She wasn't sure if he was not getting the joke, or just playing it one step further with his own expressionless answer. With his hat back on, his eyes were shaded, and it was hard to tell if he was being serious or not.

"I was really just on my way into town," she said.

"Oh. Darn shame. I was hopin' to catch you free. I wanted you to come out with me."

"Now?" Dana asked.

"Why not?" he said, shifting his weight from one leg to the other, hooking his thumbs on the belt of his Levi's.

"Well . . ." Dana said, reconsidering just how much she really needed to do that shopping in Greenleaf. "What did you have in mind? Did you want to go get an ice cream at the Tutti Frutti? See the matinee at the Rialto?"

"No. I don't have much time for that sort of thing. I have to get right back out there and tend to a few things. I just thought you might want to come with me. We could talk and I could show you around."

In making the offer, there was suddenly a nervous quavering in his voice. Maybe he wasn't as cool and in control as he seemed. Dana's heart did a little flip-flop when it occurred to her that *he* might be a little shy, too.

"Well, okay," she said and looked around. "Do we walk out there? I've got my running shoes on, so I'm prepared."

"No," he said and nodded off toward the Baker parking lot. "I've got my pickup here." He put his hand on her shoulder and began to walk her over. Just as he did this, Faith and Shelley bolted out the front door of Baker with their swimsuits thrown over their shoulders, on their way out to the falls.

As they approached, they were both giving Randy a pretty obvious once-over. Dana made introductions all around without indicating how she and Randy knew each other. She could tell they were dying of curiosity about him — not only because they didn't know who he was, but also because although they had suspected a new boy had appeared on Dana's scene, this was *not* the boy they expected. If anything, they thought she would find someone else like Bret — preppy and smooth and hip, like she was — not this lanky, dirt-smeared, cowboy-hatted boy.

Dana figured they could stay bewildered for a few more hours. This was not the time or place to explain Randy to them, and so she told them she had to get going, and let them stand there staring after her and Randy, as they walked over and got into the cab of his pickup truck, its back filled with bales of hay and sacks of manure.

If jaws really dropped like they did in cartoons, Shelley's and Faith's would have been brushing the pavement. Dana, without thinking, gave a little chuckle at this.

"You want to share the joke?" Randy said.

"Well, I think my roommates are surprised that this city girl is with a country boy."

"Will they approve?" he said, lifting her by the elbow as she climbed into the cab of the pickup.

She turned and smiled at him. "I think so."

They hadn't gone far along the highway when Randy turned off into a dirt road and kicked up clouds of dust as they barreled past miles of grazing horses, which were standing and running in small groups. Dana thought they were beautiful poetry in motion.

"Where're we headed?" she shouted over the noise of the truck and the country music blasting from the radio. Every couple of minutes, the jostling of the truck threw the music into static and Randy would have to thump the dashboard with his fist to punch it back to music again. After the third time, Dana took over as co-pilot and radio puncher.

"I've got a bit of fence to mend out here," he shouted back. "Won't take long."

They drove on for a few more minutes, then suddenly Randy turned off the road and headed uphill over a ridge on the grazing land. Just over on the other side of the ridge, he pulled the truck up and braked it by a section in the fence where the wire was down. From how easily he had found his way back to this particular section in all these miles and miles of fence, Dana could see that Randy knew this expanse of land as well as she knew her own block in New York City.

"Keep me company while I work?" he asked her while opening the rusty, creaking door on his side of the cab, then hopping down.

"Sure," Dana said and got out on her side.

It was a beautiful afternoon, with the sun white against the ultrablue New England sky, a breeze whipping across the pasture, picking up the scent of wildflowers. Dana sat down as Randy got fencing wire, heavy gloves, a hammer, and wire cutters out of the back and set to work.

One nice thing about being with a boy who doesn't talk a lot, she thought, was that she didn't have to come up with a lot of conversation herself. She was beginning to be comfortable with the silences that came up between them. She was beginning to see that they weren't nervous or awkward pauses, just places where they could be together in other ways besides talking. This was something new to her. With Bret, either he or she was always talking, or something was wrong.

"Do you need some help?" she called over to him.

"Nope. Not just now, anyhow. You can cheer me up while I work. Tell me a story."

"About what?"

"Tell me the story of your life."

Dana laughed. "How much fence have you got to mend? It's kind of a long story."

"Well then, just tell me Chapter One."

"Okay," Dana said, then thought for a minute about how to begin. "Well, I was born on February twenty-ninth, so I only have a birthday every leap year. I just turned four this year."

"Boy," Randy said. "I'm really robbing the cradle!"

"Well, look at it this way. I *am* going on five. Anyway, I was a regular baby — little and red. I've seen the pictures. I don't really remember much for the first few years. I broke my arm when I was four, falling off a jungle gym. That's the first thing I remember. The doctor set the bone and I had to wear a cast for a while."

The warm day and the light breezes and the easiness of being with Randy made Dana very relaxed. She lay back on the grass and went on with her story with her eyes shut. She didn't get much further, though, before drifting off to sleep.

When she woke, she had no idea how long she had been out, but the first thing she noticed was that the sky had changed completely. It was pale gray with dark gray clouds tumbling across it. There was a stiff wind up. She sat up with a start and looked for Randy. At first she couldn't find him. Then she turned and saw him packing the tools and wire back into the truck.

"Sudden storm," he said. "I wanted to get this fence all patched if I could, but it's coming up in a bigger hurry than I thought it would. We'd better go."

Dana made a dash for the truck, but big drops were hitting her hard by the time she got into the cab. Once inside, she was wet, shivering, and strangely scared. By now it was coming down in a torrent. All she could see out the windshield was a solid wall of water.

Randy saw that she was nervous, slid across the seat, and put his arms around her. She buried her face in the collar of his shirt. He smelled salty, not aftershavy like Bret.

Bret. Why did he keep coming up in her thoughts?

"I'm not a wimp about everything," Dana

said. "But I've been scared of storms ever since I was little. I guess my mother must've been startled by a cumulus cloud while she was pregnant with me."

It was the kind of joke Bret would have picked up on right away. Within a minute, he would have been doing impersonations of famous scary clouds — The Cloudback of Notre Dame, Frankencloud, Cloud Dracula.

Randy just said, "Nothin' to worry about."

Dana hated herself for making these comparisons. Randy wasn't Bret, wasn't trying to be Bret. He was very much his own person. He wasn't always fast and funny like Bret. So what? Sometimes it was nice to have someone gentle and serious around.

Like now. When she thought about it, did she really *want* to be joked out of her fears? Or was it nicer getting Randy's quiet reassurance?

"There's an old cabin about a mile off," he was saying. "I can get us there, even in this rain. It's not much, but it's got a stove and some wood so we can get you dry."

The rain was still coming down hard when they pulled up in front of the cabin and both of them got even wetter getting there from the truck.

"Nice place you've got here," Dana kidded him once they were inside and she'd had a chance to look around. There was an old beat-up table and a rocking chair for furniture, and a kitchen with a potbelly stove and a counter with a hand pump. The floor was weathered wood. Everything had a thick layer of dirt covering it. The windows were curtained with cobwebs.

"A hermit used to live here," Randy said, crumpling up some old sheets of newspaper to begin the fire.

"Really! Did you know him?"

"When I was a kid. He'd lived here since before we bought the land. My dad said it would be unfair to kick him off. His name was Egan. I don't know if that was his first or his last name. He only had one as far as I could tell. He was a neat guy. He taught me a lot." Now he was laying small twigs on top of the papers.

"About what?" Dana asked.

"About living out here. What you can eat, what you can't. He knew which barks could be boiled down to make medicines. For coughs. To put on cuts. He knew which berries were poisonous. Which were the good snakes, which the ones to watch out for. He taught me how to listen to the forest."

"What do you mean?" Dana said, brushing out the worst of the tangles in her sopping hair as best she could with her fingers. Randy had put small branch pieces over the tinder and lit the fire. He was standing in front of the stove, looking in, waiting for it to catch before putting bigger pieces of wood in. He turned and looked at her.

"Egan learned it from an Indian. You stand deep in the forest and wait for it to speak to you. A lot's going on in there, but most people never know about it. If you stand very still, though, and listen, and know what you're listening for, you can learn a lot about what animals are there, what weather is coming, where the food is. People think only cities are bustling. They don't know about all the action out here."

"Tell me some of the stuff Egan taught you," Dana said when he had sat down next to her in front of the fire.

He did. He talked for half an hour about birds and raccoons and elderberries and copperheads and such. She was fascinated. She had never thought about nature except in a textbook way. The way he talked about it made it seem real. She grew so absorbed that she forgot she was wet and didn't notice that the warmth from the fire had dried them off, until he mentioned it.

"I guess we can head on back now," he said, looking over his shoulder out the window. "The rain seems to have settled down to a drizzle."

His hair was stiff and matted around his head from having gotten rained on and then dried without being combed. His shirt was all wrinkly. Dana thought he looked cuter than ever mussed up like this.

She was startled to realize that she wished

he would kiss her. For ā minute, she thought he might, but then he got up and started to walk toward the stove to put out the fire.

"Ready?" he said and turned toward her.

"Ready to kiss you," she said in a flash of bravery. She grabbed him by the collar and aimed for his mouth, but he turned his head at the last second, and so she wound up planting it on his jaw. She felt like a dope, even more so when he said, "We go slower on that stuff out here in the country."

What country? What PLANET wās this guy from? Seventeen and acting like a stupid kiss was a big deal. Boy, what a hick!

"Don't think I don't appreciate the offer, though," he said and smiled at her, then pulled her into a big hug. "And you'd better watch out, 'cause I'm likely to take you up on it real soon."

Dana didn't know how she felt about this guy. One minute she liked him. The next she thought he was a total goon. It was like being in a revolving door.

She had to get away from this scene and all her confusion.

"Race you to the truck!" she said and bolted out of the cabin . . .

. . . and right into ā long patch of slick and slippery mud. She took about a four-foot skid before wiping out completely.

He responded automatically to her distress and came running after her — slipping at about the same place and falling down next to her.

They helped each other up, half falling back into the mud in the process, laughing all the while, which made it even more difficult to get up and out of the mess.

When they finally did, they looked at each other and began laughing all over again.

"Am I as big a mess as you?" she asked him.

"Worse, I think," he said and smiled. "I'd better get you back to that dorm of yours so you can get a shower."

"You know," she said as they drove back toward Canby Hall, "this is probably going to sound pretty simple-minded, but I don't think I've ever really thought much about nature, except as being pretty. Even when I came out here that day I met you, that was the angle I took for my poem."

"Well, pretty *is* one of the things nature is. But it's also powerful. And sometimes very peaceful. I like to read writers who see how complicated nature is. Thoreau. Annie Dillard. The Indians around here. The ones who taught Egan." Suddenly he stopped and looked embarrassed.

"Go on," Dana encouraged him. "I want to hear more."

"No. I don't like to talk too much at a time. Get sick of the sound of my own voice. Let's go get us a burger. If we stay in the car, only the carhop will see us. She's used to me looking like I fell into a well, but she'll be a mite surprised to see I dragged a girl in with me this time. Next time out, I promise you a clean-cut date."

A joke, Dana thought. *He can break down his seriousness and make a joke. And he laughed when he fell in the mud. And he reads about nature. Maybe there is hope for a possible romance!*

CHAPTER FOURTEEN

Faith looked up from the copy of *American Photographer* that she was reading as Dana burst into the room, covered in dried mud, carrying the remains of a sack of fries from the local burger spot.

"I'm not sure I want to know," Faith said and went back to her magazine. She, of course, was *dying* to know, but being blasé was a big part of her D.C. cool.

When Dana came back into the room twenty minutes later, scrubbed pink from her shower, Faith looked up again.

"You know, I've been thinking about your poor mother."

Dana knew a joke was on its way, so she didn't respond. This didn't stop Faith for even a second.

"Yeah, here she puts out all those bucks sending you to a cream-of-the-crop school like this, and without even talking to the vocations counselor, you decide on a career in mud wrestling."

"We fell in a mud slick," Dana said. It was the wrong place to begin the explanation.

Dana backtracked and tried to explain the mud, and then to explain Randy, and her interest in him. She told Faith how they had met, how much she liked being with him.

"But Dana," Faith said, "isn't it kind of a culture gap? I mean this isn't a TV sitcom, it's not city girl meets the cowpoke. This is real life. Do you think you have enough in common with someone like him?"

Dana looked her straight in the eye, put on her most serious expression, and set her up for a taste of her own joke medicine.

"Faith. When you've got *mud* in common, you don't need anything else."

Faith lunged off her bed and gave Dana a fast thwump with her pillow. Not one to shrink from the challenge of a pillow fight, Dana retaliated with a double thwumping of her own. Things rapidly escalated to the point where they were laughing so hard they could hardly thwump anymore. At this point, Shelley — completely unsuspecting and a little down at the mouth about Tom — came through the door and got socked by two pillows at once.

"Hey, you two. Lay off. I'm a depressed person. This will not cheer me up. It'll only make me more depressed that I am trapped in this school, being forced to live with two lunatics."

The two girls stopped and crumpled onto Dana's bed in exhaustion.

"Hey," Faith said, still out of breath, "did you look at the bulletin board when you came up? Did you see what's for dinner?"

"Yeah," Shelley said, "and you're not going to believe it. The cafeteria's closed tonight. Dinner is in the birch grove — at Patrice Allardyce's wienie roast!"

"You're kidding!" Dana said. "I can't believe it. Our prim and grim headmistress throwing a wienie roast!"

"She's probably trying to show that she's a real person," Shelley said.

"I'd need more than a wienie roast before I'd be convinced she's a human being," Faith said. "I'd have to see a blood sample."

"Aw, she was all right in the clinch when Casey tried to run away last fall," Dana remembered. "She let her off pretty easy in the end, and she got her into counseling, which has been a big help. I say let's give her a break and go down to her roast. At least it'll be food untampered with by the cafeteria staff. I assume they're going to let us roast our own wienies."

"You two go," Shelley said, "I'm too depressed to eat."

Faith looked at Dana in exaggerated disbelief.

"I must've heard her wrong," she said.

"She was probably just kidding," Dana said as if Shelley weren't there.

"If we go down without her," Faith continued, "you know she's going to be bugging us all night about how her stomach's growling, and what did we have, and was it good, until we're half crazy and have to get up and cook her a can of soup or something around three in the morning. I say it'd be easier to just drag her down to the birch grove now, and save ourselves all that trouble later."

"You're probably right." Shelley gave in right off. "As soon as I said it, I started thinking about those hot dogs. And that potato salad. And those Boston baked beans with all that molasses and bacon."

"Hey!" Dana said. "Let's get down there. I'm starving!"

It was warm and still in the birch grove. There was a large clearing in the center with a circle of felled tree trunks for seats. Usually this was used by the drama department as a theater for warm-weather performances. Tonight, where the performance would usually be, there was a roaring campfire.

A long table had been set up nearby, where raw hot dogs could be picked up for roasting on long sticks. And then the girls could come back with their charred dogs to pick up buns and all the side goodies Shelley had imagined.

The food was being served up by all the faculty, even the visiting big shots like André Rosofsky and Grace Phaeton (in a pair of striped pedal pushers Faith and Shelley were never going to let Dana forget). Even Patrice Allardyce was there, dishing out potato salad, wearing white tennis shorts and a purple Hawaiian sport shirt.

"I can't believe it!" Dana whispered, grabbing Faith by the arm when she saw this.

"Well," Faith said, "it *is* about ninety degrees tonight and we *are* out in the woods."

"Still, I would never have believed she even *owned* anything that casual. I thought she slept in a linen suit, silk shirt, and high heels."

In addition to everything else, at the end of the buffet table were the makings for S'mores.

Dana didn't know what S'mores were. Shelley, who had been a Girl Scout for five years back in Pine Bluff and had gone to any number of campfires and eaten more than her share of the world's S'mores, was amazed that anyone could not have heard of them.

"It's like not having heard of Santa Claus."

"Face it," Faith said. "The girl's culturally *over*prived. It's the opposite of *de*prived. All those years she was in New York City, watching all those plays and all that ballet and eating in all those ethnic restaurants, she missed out on a lot of the unfiner but great things in life, like S'mores. But I think it might be too late now to let her in on them."

"Come on, you two," Dana whined. "Show me what they are."

And so they took her over to the fire and got her marshmallow nice and brown on the outside, all gooey on the inside, then showed her how to pull it off between two graham crackers with a piece of chocolate stuck between them.

"See?" Shelley said. "The hot marshmallow melts the chocolate. It's the world's best sandwich."

"Mmmmm," Dana said. It was all she *could* say with a mouth full of S'more.

When everyone was through eating, Patrice Allardyce stepped into the circle, threw a couple more logs on the fire to rev it up a bit, and asked if anyone knew any camp songs.

" 'Ragtime Cowboy Joe?' " someone shouted. And so they sang it. And then "Michael Rowed the Boat Ashore." And "On Top of Old Smokey." And then they did a round of "Down by the Old Mill Stream (not the river, but the stream)." And then, there in the birch grove, they sang "The Ash Grove."

"Down yonder green valleys
Where streamlets meander . . ."

They sang the ballad in soft harmony.

When they started singing the song, all

three roommates were thinking their own separate thoughts. Dana was thinking about switching her career plans from being an architect to becoming a songwriter. She loved to sing. This past year in choir had shown her that she was better than she had thought when she was just working alone with her guitar at home. And she loved working words into images the way Grace Phaeton was having them do in the intensive. If she started putting her words and her music together and singing them . . . well, it was something to think about. Something else to think about was Randy. What was going to happen there? Were they too different? Didn't someone once say that opposites attract?

Faith was sitting next to Dana thinking about the way Johnny Bates looked in his red cotton crewneck. She was also wishing she had brought her camera loaded with that new 1,000-speed color film so she could shoot this fire with all the girls around it.

Shelley was sitting on the other side of Dana, hoping that everything would work out okay between her and Tom. She knew he was punishing her, and she figured she deserved it. But what if he found someone else during this time he was not speaking to her? Her other thought was that she wasn't going to remain the new, slim Shelley if she ate three S'mores after every meal.

By the end of the song, though, when all the girls around the campfire had crossed their arms and held hands in an unbroken chain, swaying back and forth to the lulling melody of "The Ash Grove," Dana, Faith, and Shelley were all thinking the same thought — how glad they were to be sharing whatever was going on this summer with each other.

CHAPTER FIFTEEN

When nearly a week went by and Tom still hadn't called, Shelley began to panic. She turned for advice to anyone who would give it.

"Give him a few more days," Faith said.

"Start looking around for someone new," Dana said.

"Forget about it," Casey said. "Concentrate on your acting. If you could impress André Rosofsky, maybe he'd get you a part in a Broadway play and you'd never give another thought to Greenleaf boys."

"Make him a nice pot of stew," said Marie, the cleaning woman at Baker House. "A nice stew always brings a man back home."

None of these suggestions seemed like a solution. As a last resort, Shelley approached André Rosofsky after the workshop one day.

"Buy him a rose," he told her. "A beautiful ballerina in New York did that to me by way of apology. That's twenty-five years ago now, and I still haven't forgotten it."

That was good enough for Shelley. She went into town to the Romeo and Juliet Flower Shop and got a single, long-stemmed red rose. She had the salesperson put it in a shiny black box with a wide, red satin ribbon around it. She made out a card. It didn't say anything. She just drew a small teardrop on it.

She took the box and put it in the cafeteria cold locker at Baker, then got it out at six the next morning and walked into Greenleaf and over to Tom's house. The only other person out and about at this hour was the paper boy.

As soon as he had tossed a rolled-up *Greenleaf Citizen* onto the front porch of Tom's house, Shelley followed and put the black box next to it. That way someone was sure to discover it as soon as the family was up.

She was down the block, on her way back to Canby Hall, when it hit her. There was nothing on the box to show that it was meant for Tom. Seeing that it was a flower shop box, Tom's mother would probably assume it was a present for her and open it. And then she'd ask Tom about it and he would realize who the rose was from and get all embarrassed in front of his family and probably be furious with Shelley.

This was not the romantic scenario she had in mind. And so she rushed back, fishing through the pockets of her poplin jacket as she ran, trying to find something to write on. There was nothing. She spied a fat wet maple leaf fallen from a tree on someone's lawn, picked it up, wiped it off on her jeans and then, with her Paradise Peach lipstick, wrote TOM on it in fat, greasy letters. She ran up onto the porch again. From inside, she could hear a TV blasting out one of the morning shows and someone yelling to someone else to put on the Mr. Coffee.

She knew she didn't have much time. She slid the leaf under the ribbon so that TOM showed conspicuously and then ran across the street.

Behind her, she heard the front door being opened. There was nothing to do but duck behind a big tree across the street. She peeked out from behind it to see Tom's father looking strangely at the box. He wasn't picking it up or anything, just looking at it. As if it were going to explode or something. After a moment, he prodded it with the toe of his bedroom slipper.

"Pick it up," Shelley whispered hoarsely, as if she were sending him a telepathic message. Maybe it worked, because he bent over, picked it up, shook it, and then took it inside.

Shelley waited a minute more, just to make sure the coast was clear.

"Something we can do for you, little lady?"

Shelley jumped about a foot in the air. When she came back to earth and was pretty sure she would live, even though her pulse was racing about a mile a minute, she turned and saw that the voice belonged to an older man dressed in a plaid robe and no shoes or socks. She guessed that he lived in the house that belonged to the lawn she was standing on and the tree she was hiding behind.

She knew he was going to be trouble. People who said "we" when there was only one of them, and people who asked if they could do something for you when they really meant, "What do you think you're doing on my lawn at six in the morning?" were bound to be trouble.

"No, thank you," she said, backing away ever so slowly. "I was just out of breath from my morning jog and stopped to rest against your tree." She patted the trunk of the tree to show that it was nice and sturdy to lean against. "Sorry if I was trespassing."

"You always wear those sandals when you run?" he said, pointing to her feet. "I'd think that would make it quite difficult."

"Oh, it does," Shelley nodded. "That's why I wear them. To make it even harder on my legs. Sometimes, when I really want a workout, I run in my hiking boots."

"I've been watching your *workout*. It's a pretty interesting way to get exercise, I must say." He had his hands linked behind his back and was rocking back and forth, like an interrogating detective. Shelley was getting pretty nervous.

He went on rocking and talking. "Yep. It seems to involve a lot of stops at the houses and lawns of folks in this neighborhood. Two trips up to the Stevensons' porch. Picking up something between on the Parkers' lawn. And now hiding behind my tree."

"I'm not hiding," Shelley said, trying to sound indignant. "I'm leaning. And if it's such a big deal, I'll just leave and get on my way." She started to move off.

"Just a minute, missy," the old man said. "Before you go, I think you ought to give your explanation to the police."

"Police!" Shelley said. "Oh, no. Sorry. Got to be going."

"Too late for that," the old man said, smiling. "I called them before I came out here to chat with you."

Shelley looked across the street at Tom's house. His little brother was just coming out the side door. He went into the garage, probably to get his bike.

Please, Shelley thought, *please don't let the cops have the siren on when they get here.*

Just as the thought passed through her mind, she heard it in the distance —oooo-eeeeooooeeeeqooooeeee — growing louder and louder until it was OOOOEEEEOOOOEEEE and there was the police car, rounding the corner onto Tom's block with a screech of burning rubber.

And then the cops were out of the car.

And then everyone in the neighborhood was out on their lawns.

Shelley figured her lie wouldn't get her very far with the police. She might as well tell them the whole stupid truth and get out of this mess.

"I was just trying to bring my boyfriend a flower."

The younger of the two policemen gave her a look that cops on TV shows give major criminals — bank robbers and murderers.

"Let me get this straight. *You* were bringing some *guy* a flower?"

The older cop moved in closer.

"At six in the morning? You expect us to believe that?"

"We'd better haul her in for questioning, Al," the younger one said and started to take the handcuffs off his belt.

Shelley looked up. Suddenly, there was Tom, running toward them from across the street, the black flower box underneath his arm. She smiled through the tears of fear and anxiety that were now streaming down her cheeks. The cops and the old man and the flock of neighbors who had gathered around her all turned at once to see what she was smiling at.

It took a while to resolve all the confusion. First Shelley had to explain to Tom what had happened. Then he had to convince the police and the old man that Shelley really was his girlfriend and that they'd had a fight and she was trying to apologize with a flower. He went on and on with the whole story, which was so stupid and embarrassing that they had to believe it. It took them a while, though.

Finally the younger cop pulled the older one over by the arm and said, "It's such a stupid story, it's got to be true. I think she's okay. I don't think we've caught the Greenleaf Cat Burglar."

"You thought I was the Greenleaf Cat Burglar?" Shelley shrieked, remembering all the stories of recent robberies in the local paper.

"You've got to admit you looked *mighty* suspicious," the younger policeman said. "But if your boyfriend here vouches for you, I don't think we'll have to take you in." He turned to the gathered crowd. "Now get along everybody. Go back to your breakfasts. Show's over."

"Come on," Tom said to Shelley, putting his arm around her and leading her away from the old man, who looked like he was disappointed that she hadn't been arrested and sent away for life.

Neither Tom nor Shelley said anything for a couple of blocks. They walked out of Tom's neighborhood and into the business section of Greenleaf before he turned to her and said, "Nice of you to bring by the flower. Hope you didn't have any trouble."

It took them two blocks even to begin to

stop laughing. And when they finally did stop, nobody had to say anything. At least not for the moment. There would be talk, but later. Right now it was enough for both of them that they were together again.

CHAPTER
SIXTEEN

"Hey, everybody! Grace Phaeton's going to give a reading!" Dana burst into 407 with this news bulletin.

The general response was less than overwhelming.

"That's nice," Faith said and yawned and rolled over, back into the nap she had been drifting in and out of for an hour or so.

"Yeah," Shelley agreed, and went back to her paperback copy of *King Lear*. André Rosofsky had his workshop doing scenes from Shakespeare this week, and Shelley had the part of Cordelia.

"Well, don't everybody get too excited," Dana said, petulant that her own excitement was falling so flat with her friends. This made her defensive. "You two just don't know anything about poetry. You wouldn't know a great poem if it bit you. Maybe only true students of poetry can value it properly. Everyone in the *atelier* is certainly excited about Grace's reading."

At this, Faith rolled over and opened her eyes. "I wonder if you could tell me why it is that all the other instructors are giving workshops, but Grace Phaeton is conducting an *atelier*?"

"It's a French word," Dana said.

"I *know* it's a French word," Faith said. "Even though I quit French before I could flunk the subject, I *can* usually spot a French word when I hear one. What I was trying to point out was that calling a workshop an *atelier* is pretentious, like almost everything else about Grace Phaeton."

"You'd be kinder if you knew what the poems she's reading are about," Dana said smugly.

"What?" Faith sat up. She and Dana almost never disagreed about anything, but when they did, they both felt it was better to have it out than to let it fume and foment. Faith thought Grace Phaeton was a big phony and thought Dana was being taken in by her.

"She's written a series of poems on the loneliness of being a woman poet isolated in the city."

"Oh, boy," Faith said, so exasperated that she got up, walked across the room, and gave the wall a good pounding with her fist. "If that isn't really tragic subject matter, I don't know what is. A lot of people back in my old neighborhood in Washington would really sympathize with her troubles. They don't have enough to eat or enough heat in the apartments in the winter, but they'd understand that their suffering is nothing compared with the hardships of being a poet in Manhattan."

Faith was really angry, but she was calm in comparison to Dana, who went absolutely livid at this attack on her idol. She glared at Faith from across the room. Shelley looked up from her *King Lear* in astonishment. These two might argue like crazy, but she had never seen them get into a personal fight.

"Hey," Shelley tried to intervene, "what did I miss here?"

But it was too late. Dana stormed out of the room before anyone could say anything else.

She went straight down to the pay phone and stood there a full five minutes, calming herself down enough to pick up the receiver. When she thought she was in fairly sane shape, she looked in the Greenleaf directory hanging beneath the phone on a chain.

There was only one Crowell. She dialed the number. A boy sounding just like Randy answered.

"Hi," she said, "it's Dana Morrison."

"Well, hi yourself, Dana Morrison. What can I do for you?"

"Well, I wondered if you might want to go to a poetry reading with me tonight."

"*Po*-etry reading! Hoooeee! Some girl wants to go to a poetry reading," the boy hooted and yelled and laughed. Dana was pretty sure she could even hear him stomping his feet. Then she heard him say, "Do you think this call's for Bob or Randy?" And then someone else shouted back, "Nobody inviting me to no poetry party." And then another voice, even more like Randy's saying, "I'll take that, if you guys don't mind."

"Dana?" This time it was Randy for sure. "Hi."

"Sorry about that. Brothers."

"How many do you have?"

"Five."

"Oh." She tried to imagine having five brothers. She couldn't.

"Most of the time it's not this bad. You want to start over?"

She repeated her invitation. There was such a long pause after she'd finished that she thought he was going to say no, or had put the phone down and walked off.

But then he said, "What time does the shootin' start?"

"Eight."

"Be by to fetch you at seven-thirty, then."

"Are you sure you want to do this?" she asked. She wasn't sure he was really interested, or if he even knew what a poetry reading was.

"I'm interested in seeing you. If I invited you to a tractor pull, would you come?"

Dana laughed. "Probably," she said.

"Well, there you go."

The poetry reading was scheduled to be

held in the Canby Hall auditorium, which
could hold about five hundred people. But
when Dana and Randy arrived, about ten
minutes before Grace Phaeton was due to
come on, there were only about twenty-five
people in the audience. Fifteen of them were
the other students from the poetry intensive.
The rest were a mixed lot of students, teach-
ers, some people Dana didn't recognize at
all, probably poetry lovers from Greenleaf.
There had been flyers up in the store windows all week.

Suddenly Dana felt all clenched up inside.
She had expected the place to be jammed to
the rafters, pulsing with literary excitement.
She didn't know what she had expected this
literary excitement to look like — something
like the buzz in a crowd before a really crucial basketball game, maybe — but there sure
wasn't anything like that happening here.

Here the air was filled with tension, but of
another kind, a sort of group awkwardness,
as if all of them were afraid this was going
to be a bomb and were trying to act like they
hadn't come of their own free will — that the
person next to them had dragged them in.

Programs were being folded in elaborate
shapes on laps, or crumpled and then flat-
tened out and crumpled again. People were
talking in the lowest possible whispers, as if
they were in a library or church instead of an
auditorium.

Dana realized that she had invited Randy

in hopes of impressing him with how sophisticated she was, knowing about famous poets from New York. Now, in the midst of this dismal atmosphere, she feared he would just think she was a turkey for wanting to come to something as dreary as this.

She wished they hadn't put this in the auditorium. If it were being held in one of the classrooms, it might look almost full. As it was, everyone was clustered together in the front, looking more like shipwrecked survivors on a vast deserted beach than an audience.

"Let's sit back here," Dana said to Randy, indicating a row of empty seats about halfway back. Somehow she felt that maybe the two of them sitting back there would make the auditorium look less empty.

"I guess something like this only gets those in the know," he said. She couldn't tell if he really believed this or was just being gracious. Whichever, she was grateful.

"Well, poetry never has had the pull of, say, pro football. Poets are almost never rich. Or even very famous. Not a lot of people go for it that much. I guess because it takes a little patience. It's not like reading other stuff. It doesn't step right up and shake your hand and tell you what it means."

"Why not?" Randy asked, looking at her sincerely so Dana could tell he wasn't trying to hassle her, just trying to understand.

"I guess because it's trying to affect you,

not just give you information. I mean it's trying to say something in the most beautiful way, or the most powerful, or whatever. It's not just trying to tell you how to fix your carburetor."

He laughed a little at that.

"Well, guess I'm as ready as I'll ever be," he said and rolled his program into a tight tube and leaned forward with his arms on his thighs and stared at the stage.

It was as if Grace Phaeton, waiting backstage, felt the force of his waiting. The lights in the auditorium dimmed and the ones on the stage came up and she walked out to the lectern in the center of the stage's highly polished wood floor.

Dana's spirits lifted. Maybe Randy would get behind her in her love of poetry where Faith and Shelley had failed her.

Grace Phaeton was, Dana had to admit, really dressed on her own wavelength tonight. She looked dramatic and exciting in a striped silky dress over gauzy harem pants. On one arm, she was wearing heavy silver bracelets that jangled slightly. Her hair fell in wild waves that caught the light.

Dana looked over at Randy, but he was still just staring ahead intently. Whatever he was thinking, he wasn't letting on.

Onstage, Grace Phaeton shuffled her typewritten sheets of poems for what seemed like forever, then took a drink from the glass of water on the lectern, then shuffled the pages

some more, then went through half a dozen
pockets until she came up with her eye-
glasses. The audience was growing restless,
coughing, looking around, beating their programs against their legs in time to songs running through their heads.

Finally Grace cleared her throat and began:

"Trudging to the laundromat on Saturday
night . . ."

and ended an hour later with

". . . put my soul in the elevator and pushed
the Basement button."

Dana felt absolutely wiped out. Grace
Phaeton had really outdone herself this time.
What did it matter if no one was here? Their
loss. She was still a genius, with or without
an audience.

Dana turned to Randy.

"Well," she said, hoping to get a comment
on the performance from him. But he didn't
say anything, just looked at her as if he were
expecting her to say something else.

"What do you want to do now?" she tried.

"I think the only thing we *can* do is kill
ourselves." He smiled to show he was kidding. Dana hated herself for having thought
he was different.

"You!" she said, getting up out of her seat

as fast as she could. "You're just like the rest of them!"

She ran out of the auditorium and across the campus to the cinder running track, then did laps around it until she was winded and had a terrible stitch in her side from running and crying at the same time.

The clod, she thought. *The dolt*. She'd been a fool to think they had enough in common. Let him go back to his friends — the squirrels and the otters.

Of course, what had she expected to find up here in the woods? The problem wasn't him — this was *his* turf. It was she who was in the wrong place — isolated, alienated, just like Grace Phaeton. Dana was a poet alone in the country.

Suddenly she was overcome with longing for home, for Manhattan — for good ballet and funky flea markets and high-rise apartments with dynamite views and hot dogs piled high with sauerkraut.

And she also longed for Bret. He was the person up here who really understood her best, appreciated her most. They thought alike on so many subjects that it was eerie. They liked the same music, the same movies, the same jokes. They even liked the same stuff on their pizzas!

She wondered if she could ever hope for this kind of rapport with Randy. Maybe she should just throw in the towel on this budding romance.

CHAPTER SEVENTEEN

The next night Casey went down to the cafeteria early and came up to 407 ten minutes later with the report.

"They've got something down there called Sahara Surprise. Amy Jennings was behind me in line and she said she heard it was fried camel. It looked a little like fried camel. It kind of had humps."

"They can't serve camel in this country, can they?" Shelley wondered aloud.

Casey arched an eyebrow. "Do you want to take the chance? I say tonight's the night to shake out the piggy banks, empty the coffers, spend the allowances, and order a humongous pizza!"

"Oh, yeah!" Faith agreed. "I can get behind that!"

"Uh-oh," Shelley said. "I went into town this afternoon and bought two lipsticks and a tube top for tanning. I've only got — let's see — a dollar and fourteen cents left."

"Shel!" Faith said and sighed with exasperation. "This always happens. It's as if you *know* when we're going to order a pizza. You go out and spend all your money, and then we let you in anyway and you eat half the pizza yourself."

"I'll only eat two pieces, I promise."

"Okay," Faith said, then turned to Dana, who was reading a book of Emily Dickinson's poetry, making a point of staying out of the discussion.

"Dana?" Faith said, trying to get her attention. "What say?"

"Oh," Dana said, as if her mind had just landed from another planet, "no thanks. I'm not very hungry. I'll probably just go downstairs later and hit the salad bar." This was partly true. Yesterday's blow-ups with Faith and Randy had left her pretty much without an appetite. The other part was that she didn't want to have anything to do with Faith until she apologized. Which probably wasn't going to happen soon. Faith, especially when backed into a corner, often ducked the issue until she could find a way to both say she was sorry and save face.

And so Dana was surprised when Faith, standing in the middle of the room, looked hard at her and said, "Step outside for a second, pardner?" — imitating a million saloon-fight scenes from cowboy movies.

Dana smiled in spite of the tension in the

room and said, "Sure." And she followed Faith into the hallway.

Faith put a hand on Dana's shoulder. "I've been thinking," she said. "I don't always do that so well, I guess. I don't think I was thinking at all yesterday. I was just a jerk to get on you about your poet lady. I don't think much of her, it's true, but that doesn't mean I should hassle you because you *do*. It's a matter of taste, and my thinking is that friends should allow each other those kinds of differences. Or at least be able to say *I think your taste stinks, but I still love you.*"

Dana just stood there, taking in what Faith was saying. Faith was impatient, though, for some response.

"So," she said, "I'm sorry. Really."

Dana still didn't say anything. And so Faith began again.

"Here I am, begging thy forgiveness," she said in a high-drama voice, like the one Shelley used for her Cordelia in *King Lear*.

The only possible response to this was to laugh, which Dana did. She was still laughing when Alison came out of the stairwell door and spotted them. She came over.

"Why do I have the feeling I came in way too late on this joke?" she said, then handed Dana a heavy white envelope. "Some guy who looks like he stepped out of an L. L. Bean catalog dropped this off for you. You know who I mean — Mr. Rugged Outdoors?"

"I've got a pretty good idea," Dana said, but decided to be a little mysterious with Alison, and left it at that. She took the envelope and walked down the hall toward the broom closet, which was usually the only place on the floor where a girl could get any real privacy.

Once inside, she pulled the door shut until there was just a crack of light coming in. Then she sat down next to the vacuum cleaner and opened the envelope. She was expecting a dumb letter — some kind of clumsy apology, or a note telling her she was cute as a spotted hound dog when she was mad — not this. It was a poem.

> I talk a good game.
> Tell you about listening to the forest
>   then I turn around and tromp
>   right over your feelings.
> Egan would cry.
>
> Would you give me a chance
> to make it up to him
> and to you?

It was printed in big bold letters in heavy black fountain-pen ink on lined notebook paper. There was no signature. Dana didn't need one.

She sat there astounded. How could she have been so wrong? She'd only been looking at the surface. If he wasn't from the big city and wasn't a nonstop talker and charmer, then he must just be a dumb, insensitive hick. Rereading the poem, she felt ashamed at her shallowness. She knew that anyone who could write this had a lot going on inside himself.

She folded the poem, slipped it back in its envelope, and stuck it into the back pocket of her jeans, then headed down the back stairs, which let out onto the parking lot.

She was right. He was there, leaning back against the side of his pickup, his hat pulled down over his eyes.

"It's the first poem anyone has ever written me," she said when she got to him.

"It's the first one I ever wrote," he said, taking off his hat and tossing it over his shoulder through the open window onto the seat. "I'm not claiming it's any good."

"I'll never know," Dana told him. "I like it too much to do anything but like it."

"And what about the writer of the poem?" he said, seriousness in his eyes.

"Well," Dana said shyly, "the poem showed me a lot about him I didn't know. I think I'm beginning to see who he really is now. And I like what I see."

He grinned that slow grin of his and said, "I do believe I'd like to collect on that offer of a kiss now."

She smiled teasingly, "They only allow hand-holding on campus."

"Hand-holding! Aw, shucks!"

"Aw, shucks?" Dana said. "Do you country boys *really* say that? What about *pshaw*? What about *tarnation*?" She started tickling him around the ribs. *"Dadburned? As the crow flies? Knee-high to a grasshopper?"*

For some reason, it was the last one that did it, and Dana suddenly found herself being chased across campus by a very long-legged country boy. But Dana was the runner and kept ahead of him all the way into the birch grove, where she slowed down enough to let him catch up with her.

"I should tell you," she said breathlessly as he ran up and pulled her into his arms, "that the no-kissing rule is the most broken one at Canby Hall."

CHAPTER EIGHTEEN

Dear Paul (a.k.a. Honeybear),
(better scratch that, he hasn't called you Honeybunch in his last two letters)

Dear Paul,
I'm sorry you decided not to go to an Ivy League school. It would be fun having you out here.
(cross that out — having him and Tom around at the same time would probably make you have a nervous breakdown)

Dear Paul,
So you've decided on Drake. I've heard it's a good school. I'm a little surprised you're staying in Iowa, though, when there's a whole big world out here to explore.
(forget it, too preachy)

Dear Paul,
I'm sorry you're so negative about my

144

switching my career interest from home ec
to drama. I understand that it's more *realistic*
to plan on becoming a homemaker than becoming an actress, but that's not enough to
stop me from trying.
(*phooey, why am I justifying my career
choice to him?*)

Hey Paul,
    Go jump in the lake.
    (*a little on the hostile side?*)

Paul,

    "Hey!" Dana said, coming in and seeing
all the crumpled sheets of paper on the floor
around Shelley's desk. She looked at the
latest draft in the typewriter and said, "I
think the Declaration of Independence was
written in fewer drafts than this."
    Shelley thought for a moment.
    "I guess that's what this is, sort of. *My*
declaration of independence. If we're going
to go on — as boyfriend and girlfriend, even
just as friends — he has to know who I am,
and like me, not want me to be who I'm not
anymore."
    "Hoooray for Shel!" Faith rolled over and
shouted in a muffled way.
    Dana and Shelley looked over, then at each
other.
    "I thought she was asleep," Dana said.
    "She is, I think," Shelley said. "Sometimes

she sort of connects with the real world, even from Napland. When she starts talking in her sleep, you can sometimes keep her going in a conversation."

"Hey, Faithy," Dana shouted, "time to go down to the *deeelicious* cafeteria!"

"Hooray," Faith said in a dead, foggy monotone.

"Definitely asleep," Dana said.

CHAPTER NINETEEN

Dana, Faith, and Shelley were sitting out under their favorite tree on Sunday afternoon. It was a huge old elm way out by the skating pond. Not too many of the girls went there in the summer and so the roommates used it as their private meeting spot.

Today they had sneaked peanut butter and jelly sandwiches out of the cafeteria, bought chips and milk from the machines in the basement, and brought everything out here for a picnic lunch.

When they had finished eating, Faith got to work on a cotton sweater vest she'd been crocheting all summer. Shelley was reading the comics in the Sunday edition of the *Greenleaf Citizen*.

"You two want to go into town tonight and catch a movie?" Faith asked.

"Okay by me," Shelley said, not looking up from the paper.

"Dana?" Faith pressed.

147

"Huh?"

"Movie? Tonight? Us?"

"Oh. Better count me out. I want to stick around the room and try to maintain an alpha-level poetry energy-gathering state."

"I'll do a rough translation on that for you, Shel," Faith said. "I think what the girl means is that she wants to stick around the room tonight in case she gets a call from that guy who smells like his horse."

Dana knew Faith was only teasing, and took the remark good-naturedly.

"You know," she told them, "I'm just as bewildered by this relationship as you two are. I mean, I realize that we could hardly be less alike. I mean *I* like Chopin and the Stones. *Randy's* idea of hot music is picking bluegrass on his guitar. *I* like northern Italian restaurants in Manhattan. To *him*, gourmet cooking is pot roast and scrapple."

"Scrapple?" Faith said.

"Don't ask me," Dana said. "I haven't found out what it is yet. He talks about it all the time, though. It's some old New England specialty. Can you imagine me bringing him to my favorite sushi bar in New York? Can you imagine me trying to get him to eat raw fish?"

"I can't imagine you taking him anywhere indoors," Faith said. "He's usually got so much mud caked on those boots of his, it seems best to keep him outdoors. I wonder what he does in the winter."

"I know you're hardly even exaggerating," Dana said. "But the thing is that I like him. I do! He may not be going to college, but he's read twice as many books as I have. A lot of them about nature and the outdoors. Stuff I haven't even thought about. He may not be Mr. Smooth Talk like Bret, but when he *does* say something, it's smart and clearsighted and from an angle I hadn't even thought of. And he's sensitive to me. He knows what I'm thinking and feeling before I even tell him. And he *cares* about me."

"And he's *really* cute," Shelley said. "Of course, *I'm* partial to farm boys."

"I must admit," Faith said, "I find him rather adorable myself. And I'm a city girl."

"So you two approve of this?" Dana said, a little amazed, after all the teasing she'd been taking from them about city girl-country boy stuff.

"Oh, Dana," Shelley said, "of course. You're so happy these days."

"Not just happier than you were *without* Bret," Faith said, "happier than you were *with* him. I think that part of what you felt for Bret was being linked with one of the most popular guys from Oakley. With Randy, I think you like him purely for himself."

"Faith," Dana said, smiling, "I think you might have just hit the nail on the head."

But she could only hold on to this certainty about her and Randy until that night, when he *did* call and they got together for an ice cream at Tutti Frutti.

The place was packed with kids. About the only space they could find was a booth in the front window. Nobody really liked these as every passerby could look in at you.

Dana held on to the booth while Randy went up to the counter to order for them. He came back with one giant sundae — a King Kong, seven scoops of ice cream surrounded by bananas and topped with a little paper Empire State Building. He also had two spoons. He slid in next to her so they were sitting on the same side of the booth.

They were having a good time. He was beginning to relax with her, and was telling funny stories about life in a family of boys. Dana was so absorbed in Randy and the sundae that she didn't notice Bret until he was almost on top of them, standing right next to the booth, grinning his friendliest smile.

"Hi," he said to Dana, then turned to Randy and stuck out his hand. "Bret Harper."

Randy, socially ambushed, awkwardly positioned in the small booth, and caught with a mouth full of bananas, said what sounded like "Mmmffwoofmmf," but was probably "Randy Crowell. Glad to meet you."

He stood up as he said this. Or tried to. He moved so fast that he didn't see the hanging fern above him before he hit it with his head.

While he was reaching up, trying to quiet it down — it was bouncing around like a punched punching bag — he realized that the napkin he'd stuck into his belt was dangling like a miniature waiter's apron. He quickly pulled it out.

Dana was dying of embarrassment just watching him, then went into double death when she looked up and saw Bret smirking.

"Mind if I sit down with you?" Bret said innocently. He was holding a small, neat, single-dip cone. He was, as usual, clean and pressed to the point where he looked like he was posing for a men's fashion ad. Randy, by comparison, in his old jeans, plain white T-shirt, and workboots, looked like he had just ridden in and parked his horse outside.

"There doesn't seem to be a free inch of space in here," Bret went on. But Dana knew he wasn't just looking for a place to sit. She knew in a flash that he was here to give Randy the once-over. He had apparently heard that Dana was seeing someone new, and wanted to check him out.

"So, Randy," Bret said, sliding into the seat opposite them. "I don't think I've seen you around Oakley. You go to Greenleaf High?"

"Did," Randy said. "I'm out now."

"Oh, a college man," Bret said.

"Nope. I'm through with school now."

"Interesting. You know, historically, a lot of famous people were dropouts."

"Bret," Dana said sharply. "*Dropout* refers to people who quit in the middle of high school. College is still optional, I believe."

"Not according to my dad," Bret said, shaking his head. "If I decided not to go to college, I can't even imagine what he'd say."

"Yeah," Randy said. "Mine's none too happy about it, but I'm my own man now, I figure. I'm tired of being cooped up in a classroom. I'm an outdoors guy and I need to be out-of-doors."

"Well, then," Bret said, an impish grin on his face, "I can see why you're with Dana. She's a real outdoors girl."

"She is?" Randy said, not seeing the joke coming.

"Sure," Bret said. "Back home she had to go outdoors to get in a taxi, then outdoors again to get from the taxi into Bloomingdale's."

Dana couldn't help laughing. It was the kind of teasing joke that Bret used to make her laugh with all the time. His pulling her leg now made her feel close to him again.

But Randy didn't see this. He was only looking at Bret. Suddenly he was very red in the face. He started to stand up, then eyed the hanging fern and thought better of it. Instead, he leaned across the table and grabbed Bret by the starched collar of his oxford-cloth shirt.

"Don't you go sayin' anything smart-mouthed about my girl, you hear?"

Bret looked down at Randy's fist on his collar as if it were a worm.

"Look, fella," Bret said. "I forgot to bring my boxing gloves tonight, so why don't we just let it go, okay?" He slid out of the booth and started to go, then stopped and turned back to Randy. "And buddy, if I were you, I'd watch who you called *your* girl. If I know this one" — here he looked long and hard at Dana — "and I think I do, she doesn't like to be thought of as anyone's private property. She's an independent woman."

With this he smiled and left.

"I gather," Randy said when Bret was out of the shop, "that you used to know that guy pretty well."

"Yeah," Dana admitted. "He was my boy-friend, before I met you."

"Are you still in love with him?"

"Randy! What a thing to say!"

"Is it?" Randy said and looked deep into her eyes. "Is it really? I'm not so sure about that. I may not be the world's greatest talker, but I'm a pretty good observer, and I can tell you that while he was at this table, it was pretty hard for me to tell which of us you liked."

And with that, he got up and walked out.

Dana sat there stunned for several min-utes. Then a large, giggling party of girls carrying banana splits came up. One of them said, "Hey. Are you done? Do you mind if we sit here? I mean, are you waiting for someone?"

"I don't think so," Dana said, and embarrassingly burst into tears.

CHAPTER TWENTY

The next day Danā was sitting out on the bleachers facing the running track. After running and doing her stretching exercises, she had pulled her small notebook out of her pocket and sat down to begin the latest poetry assignment. This time they were supposed to write about an important relationship in their lives. After yesterday, she couldn't bear to think, much less write, about either of her boy relationships. And so, she was going to write about her sister, Maggie, whom she loved a lot and felt extremely protective toward.

She was trying to think back to the beginning with Maggie, who was two years younger than Dana. Family legend had it that when they brought Maggie home from the hospital, jealous little Dana had been found pinching her in her crib. Soon after that, though, Dana had taken to the new baby, and her affection had continued through the years — except for the time she had caught Maggie and one of her friends reading Dana's diary.

She was going to write about vacation trips in the car that they used to take when her mother and father were still married, when the whole family was still together. She and Maggie shared the backseat for those long days of driving through farmland and small towns and hills and along the Atlantic shore on the way to famous sights and monuments.

She was deep in these memories when a shadow fell across her notebook page. She looked up. It was Bret, standing in front of the bleachers.

She was astonished and flustered and happy and furious all at the same time. She knew that Randy had been right. As badly as Bret had treated her and as far from her as he had run, she was still, at least in part, hung up on him.

"Busy?" he asked her.

"Writing a poem," she said. She didn't dare say anything more for fear of exploding with all her feelings at once.

"Oh, yeah? How's your intensive going?"

"Bret, please. Let's not make small talk. Last night you show up in my life. And now today again. Something's going on and I want to know what it is."

He shifted around from foot to foot nervously and stuffed his fists in the pockets of his crisply pressed khakis.

"I think I'm going to need a little time to

ease into this," he said and smiled his most charming smile. She looked at him hard. He was still outrageously handsome. One in a thousand. His black hair still fell all over his head in tiny, shiny feathers. His eyes were still as deep as lagoon pools. His smile was still a toothpaste ad.

While she gazed at him, he continued to move restlessly. When he finally found words, they were: "I've been thinking about you lately, and I realize I was pretty rotten to you."

"That's a fact," Dana said, hurting with the memory. "You were."

"And I just want you to know I'm sorry for being a jerk."

Dana could tell it was hard for him to say this. Bret was not big on admitting he was wrong.

"Apology accepted," she said.

"Really?" he said as if amazed that it would be this easy.

"Sure," Dana said. "I don't want to be mad at you. You were the person I was closest to all last year. It's been real weird not talking to you."

"It has, hasn't it?" he replied. "Can you talk to *him* like that?"

"Randy?"

"Yeah," Bret said. "Superhick."

"Bret," Dana stopped him. "I can't let you talk about him like that."

"Okay, okay," Bret said, "but tell me, do

you have the same kind of closeness with him that *we* had? Do you?"

Dana grew confused. It was one thing for Bret to turn up here to apologize. She had hoped for this for weeks. But this was something else. She tried to express her feelings as best she could.

"Bret, I don't think you have any business waltzing up here and demanding an account of my relationship with Randy. They're two different things. Randy's present. You're in my past."

"But what if I came into your present?"

Dana grew even more confused. "What are you saying — that you want to be friends?"

He moved toward her, then bent one knee and knelt on the bleacher in front of her. He took her hand.

"I was thinking maybe more than friends," he said.

"But what about Renée?" Now Dana was *really* confused.

"Her mother's sick. She's going to have to go back to France. It wasn't working out all that well anyway, to tell you the truth."

"Wait a minute," Dana said. "Let me get this straight. You dump me and start up with Renée. Then you decide you don't like her. And you also don't like *me* having a new boyfriend. And so here you are at the old running track. Oh, Bret!"

"Wait, honey, it's not like that." (At the sound of him calling her "honey" like he used to, Dana melted a little in spite of herself.) "It's just taken me a while to get my head together and see things clearly. I'd like to give it another try, if you would."

"But until when — until the next interesting exchange student comes along, the next giggly blonde, the next brilliant redhead?"

Bret got a very serious look on his face. "Dana, I can't make promises for us living happily after. Nobody can. All I can say is that I'd like to give us another try and see what happens." He stopped for a minute, then said, "I've missed you."

She knew she should tell him to get lost, to take a long walk off a short pier. She knew, too, that she was right about *why* he was suddenly back, no matter what he said. He didn't like not having a girlfriend and really didn't like her having a new boyfriend, and so here was his perfectly childish solution.

Still, whatever his reasons, he *was* here. Bret. Whom she'd cried for all those nights, waited for all those days. All she had to say was yes and she could have him back.

She still partly loved him. She knew that. Looking at him now, Dana thought that in some way, she would always love him.

But now there was Randy. Her feelings for him were different. Newer, for one thing. She couldn't be sure that the beginning they had would grow into something as close as she had had with Bret. But maybe it could grow into something even better.

After last night, of course, Randy might never even speak to her again. She was hoping she could break through the barrier of his silence, though. She figured this time it was her turn to apologize. She'd been planning to run out to his place this afternoon. Now . . . now she just didn't know.

"Well?" Bret said.

"I just don't know. I can't seem to think straight at the moment. I'll need some time."

"Well, you don't have much. Intensives are over tomorrow. Wednesday's the big finale and then we all head home for the long summer. If I haven't heard from you by then, I'll just have to assume you're not interested in me anymore," he said petulantly.

"I'll have to think about it," Dana said, her stomach in knots. "I just can't say anything more than that now."

"Have it your way," Bret said bitterly, and walked off.

CHAPTER TWENTY-ONE

The intensives finished off with a giant presentation of the work done in them — an all-day extravaganza held in the Canby Hall auditorium. It was called the Canby-Oakley Multi-Media Celebration.

Everyone was excited about it. Families and friends were coming up. It was both fun and scary to be showing off everything they'd been doing for the past month.

Up in 407 that morning, Shelley was practicing her Cordelia. Faith's family had arrived and she had taken them down to the lobby of the auditorium, where her assemblage of leaf photos had been give an entire wall. They were already the stars of the photo intensive exhibit.

Shelley broke from rehearsing and noticed that Dana was putting on her running gear. *Running gear?*

"Dana — isn't it a little late for that now?"

"I'll be back in time," Dana said. "Don't worry." And then she was gone.

Shelley stared at the doorway Dana had just rushed out of and was mystified. She knew Dana had been going through a couple of days of inner torment — trying to decide between Bret and Randy. As far as Shelley and Faith were concerned, the choice was easy — Randy. They just wished Bret would move to Tibet or someplace that far away, and quit jazzing Dana up. But Shelley didn't feel it was her place to say that. What she did say yesterday — since she now felt she was the world's leading expert on how *not* to handle this situation — was that whichever way Dana decided, the important thing was that she *did* make up her mind.

Shelley guessed that Dana's rush out of the room meant that she *had* made up her mind, but which way, Shelley couldn't guess.

Shelley had her own problems to worry about at the moment. She wanted her Cordelia to be perfect for her family and for Tom, who had promised to be there early to get a front-row seat.

As it turned out, it was far from perfect. It might have been the first time in its history that this particular scene from *King Lear* brought down the house with laughter.

The culprit was a cardboard pillar behind Shelley that started to lean precariously during one of her speeches. To keep it from toppling entirely, she had to hold it up with one hand through the entire rest of the scene.

She took this disaster pretty well. Afterward she told everyone, "Even Sarah Bernhardt had these kinds of things happen to her. André says the test of a great actress is that she can ride the waves of fortune — and misfortune."

It also helped that, after the performance, André Rosofsky told her that she was the most promising high school student he had ever coached. And that he wanted to see her in his workshop in New York as soon as she graduated.

Bret was not in any of the dance performances, which led Faith and Shelley to surmise that Dana had run back into his arms and was there at this very moment. In the meantime, Dana's mother and her sister, Maggie, had arrived from New York and were clearly upset that Dana was not around to meet them and sit with them through the drama and dance segments.

The two roommates came up with the best excuse they could.

"She's real nervous about her poem," Shelley told them. "The one she's going to read."

"Yeah," Faith said. "She's off in her secret place right now, putting the finishing touches on it. She said she hoped you'd understand — that she wanted to get it right so you'd be proud of her."

This seemed to settle them down.

If Bret was conspicuously absent from the dance segment, Casey Flint was noticeably present. She stunned everyone by performing a piece she'd been keeping secret for weeks, one she'd choreographed herself. She called it "True Starts." In it, she interpreted in movement the beginning and stopping and thinking and beginning again that she felt her adolescence was all about.

Dana still wasn't back when the poetry segment began. An unexpected participant in it was Ronald Stillwell. After getting tossed out by Grace Phaeton, he had tried to go home, but the Oakley headmaster stuck to instructions from Ronald's parents that under no circumstances was he to be allowed to go home until they were back there.

He had tried to get into another intensive, but they were all full. And so he had no choice but to apologize to Grace Phaeton and ask her to let him back in. Which she did, but with one stipulation — that he work only on comic poetry.

The result was the poem he read today. It was called "Two Hundred Clorets" and was about a guy's worries before going out on his first date. By the time he was finished reading, the audience was howling.

After three more students read their poems, Dana had still not shown up. There was a temporary lag in the program, and then, after five minutes or so, Grace Phaeton came onstage.

"Excuse me," she said nervously, "but we have a change in the program. Dana Morrison will now read, not 'Wind and Leaves' as planned, but a new poem called" — here she paused and peered at a notation she'd made on the back of her program — "'Lessons from Egan.' "

Dana came out onstage and began reading:

> Confusion
> Bright lights. Night lights.
> Red lights. Green lights. Blue lights
>   from tempting eyes.
> Lost in the city of my heart.
>
> And so I ran into the forest
> And sat very still
> And listened
> And waited for it to give me a poem.
>   Instead it gave me you.

At this, she looked to the back of the auditorium. Faith and Shelley, the only ones who knew what this poem was really about, turned around in their seats and saw Randy standing there against the back wall, his hat in his hand, smiling back at Dana. She must have run all the way out to his place this morning.

Suddenly, there was a small stirring in the audience on the other side of the auditorium. It was Bret, climbing over everyone in his row in a rush to get out. They couldn't see his face from their seats up front, but they could imagine the expression on it.

When the celebration was over, everyone headed out to the big open meadow at the edge of campus for a big, old-time New England picnic supper with ham and chicken and potato salad and corn pudding and even scrapple. (Randy and Dana shared a secret smile over this.)

That night, the last night before they were all going home, the three girls sprawled on their beds in their room. Dana sighed and said, "What a month! What a day!"

"Although I approve of your decision," Shelley said, "I'm interested to know how you made it."

"It's pretty much like I said in the poem. When I sat very still and really listened to what was going on inside me, I knew that Randy was the one I wanted. Even though we're different. Even though it's just beginning and I'm not really sure where it will go. But I do know he's honest, gentle, kind, loving, sensitive. And that Bret — as much fun as he is, as much as he can make me laugh, as romantic as his gestures are — will never be able to stick with it. Two weeks from now or two months, someone new will turn his head and he'll be off again. I'll always have a soft spot for him, but I think I'd like to get off his roller coaster."

"I'm glad you got it all straightened out in your head," Faith said. "It sure *has* been an *intense* time. And today — well, even old sarcastic, cynical me has to say it's been one of the most exciting days of my life."

"And it was so neat at the picnic," Shelley said. "All our families getting together. And our boyfriends. I think everybody really liked each other, too. You know, I looked at my family and then over at you two and I realized that . . . well . . . that I've come to think of you as my family, too."

"Same here, Shel," Faith said.

They talked about their plans for the rest of the summer, hating to stop talking and go to sleep, hating to be separating the next day.

"I'm sure going to miss you guys," Dana said sadly.

"Me too," Faith agreed.

"*Moi aussi*," Shelley said proudly. "That means 'me too.' "

"We know, Shel," Dana said, smiling.

Suddenly Shelley jumped up. "I've got a brilliant idea."

"Uh-oh," Dana mumbled.

"Why don't you two come and visit *me* the last two weeks in August. My folks would love it. Say yes . . . after I check with my parents."

Dana thought for a moment. "I'm sure it would be okay with my mother, but I'd have to call her."

Faith nodded. "My mom will think it's fine,

too. I know it. . . . But I'd better check, too."

Shelley said, "*Now*! Everyone to the phones and then back here."

The three of them ran down to the pay phones and, by one of those one-in-a-million strokes of luck, were all able to reach their mothers. Dana and Faith got back to the room before Shelley.

"It's okay with my mother," Dana said. "I think she's glad she won't have to worry about what I'll be doing those two weeks."

"My mom says it's fine with her, too," Faith said.

Now that their mothers had agreed to the trip, both girls were nervous about two weeks in a completely strange place.

"Maybe Shelley's parents will say no," Dana said, almost hopefully.

But the girls *knew* it would be okay with the Hydes.

"What have we gotten ourselves into?" Dana asked in a low voice. "How do we know we'll like it?"

Faith shrugged. "Well, at least we'll all be together."

Dana smiled. "You're right. *Together*, the way we should be."